THE APOCRYPHA OF THE APOCALYPSE

Collected Stories & Prose

by

SUZI M

XIRCON

JAMES GLASS

&

MR. MINISTRY

Smiling Goth Productions

www.SmilingGoth.com

ISBN-13: 978-1463688325

First edition paperback 2013.

Book Cover Design by Robert W. Cook, http://www.norot-art.com/

Acknowledgements: Thank you to the readers of the world.

Author pages:

Suzi M: https://www.facebook.com/SuziMOfficial

Xircon:

https://www.facebook.com/pages/Xircon/184383301713608

James Glass: https://www.facebook.com/JamesRGlassII

Additional Titles Available at: http://www.amazon.com/Suzi-M/e/B003TTLGP2/ref=ntt_athr_dp_pel_pop_1

THE APOCRYPHA OF THE APOCALYPSE

SCARRED

By Suzi M

Staring at your own headstone is no way to start the evening, most people will tell you. Depending on the time and circumstances, I find staring at your own epitaph on your custom-made grave marker can really put your night in perspective. Nothing says you wasted your life quite like the old cliché 'so-and-so will be missed' sort of thing that distantly related relatives will slap onto that piece of rock. And if I have not yet had my cup of coffee to wake me up before staring at the hard gray truth… well, that makes for a shitty night for everyone.

I kicked my feet up onto the scarred surface of my desk-- an ancient wooden model with drawers that protested doing their built in duty more than a john paying for a trick. Staring at the tips of my shoes, I considered polishing them up for a more professional appearance; then decided it would be easier to just get a new pair of shoes. Ones without holes in the soles and along the uppers. From my reclined position I could still make out the curved top of my tombstone lurking in the shadows. I pulled open the bottom drawer of the desk and decided the best thing to do to set things right would be to American up my whiskey with a shot of coffee.

This is usually around the time that the hot chick walks into the noir detective's office and flounces more tit and ass than a guy can say no to, but I am sadly not that noir detective nor would the tactic work. I look good in a suit, sure, but I like the men. On an optimistic note, I am told that it is fairly normal behavior for women to feel that way. Whatever passes for normal, anyway. I am sure I still pass for a woman, but beyond that, I am totally at a loss.

Coming back from the dead was my first mistake. Going back to work instead of cashing out my sick days was my second mistake. Afterall, death was a very plausible excuse for not going to work. I think they may even give more time off if the person who died is you. As I said before, I am sadly not a noir detective, and this is not a noir detective story. I refuse to go sleuthing amongst the offices of human resources to find out how much time off I should be taking to mourn my own passing.

I could hear footsteps in the dingy hallway outside my office door, and then in walked a very agitated model of masculinity. His eyes darted here and there, then fell onto my desk and its little placard with my name and title.

"What can I do for you?" I asked casually while lighting a cigarette.

He looked to protest my smoking and I arched an eyebrow that said 'now was not a good time to talk about my bad habits.' I sucked in a breath and blew the smoke away from us, not that it helped in the small office.

"This is going to sound crazy," he started.

"You died. From the looks of you, I'd say it was by car accident."

He looked amazed. "Yes."

"And now you're wondering what the hell you're doing back amongst the air-breathers."

"Yes!"

"Mmmmm-hmmm."

"How did you know?"

I nodded to my own gravestone, squinting against the smoke. "Join the club, Hon. I've been getting calls off the hook since I came back."

He seemed genuinely disturbed by my office decoration. I have to admit, I could not remember how I had gotten the thing from my grave and into the office with me. Something in the back of what I assumed were my now maggots for brains told me I really should not investigate further into my demise; nor should I try to solve this undead Honey's case.

"Do you know what happened to us?"

"Nope. Not a clue."

"Will you find out for me? I need to know what's going on."

"Sorry, guy, I have my own worries. Since the resurrection I've decided to live a much more in the now life. That means I don't worry about the past, and I don't think about the future."

"I can pay…."

It sounded almost like a question, I had to smirk. I shook my head as I dropped my beat up shoes off my beat up desk and onto an even more beat up floor.

"Money's passé. I'm not quite sure what happened, but I don't want to know."

He stared at me as if I had died and come back from the grave. I sucked another drag off my cancer stick and regarded him for a moment, regretting my choice even before the words were out of my mouth. I have always been a sucker for blue-eyed frat boys and a man in uniform.

"Fine. I'll see what I can do."

In the end it all turned out to be a fluke. The dead started to drop off again and were quickly buried in vaults that were sealed. Accusations about government experiments flew, but no country stepped up to take the blame for it, and so there was no donkey on which to pin the proverbial tail.

Blue Eyes came back to my office looking hopeful. My poker face is not a good one, and he quickly got the idea that I had some bad news.

"Sorry," I began, "No answers…. We're just an accident."

"What does that mean?"

"Means we'll be sorted out in about a day or two."

"Huh?"

"We'll be taking another dirt nap again real soon."

"How do you know?"

"Because I broke a tooth trying to bite into someone's skull.... This isn't the movies. We're starving back to death."

"Shit."

"Indeed."

ENOCH'S DEVIL

By Suzi M

In retrospect, he realized he should have known better. Hot women did not normally pay attention to him unless he was buying their drinks or their company for the evening. He was unremarkable in the most unremarkable ways, so when the blonde woman whispered in his ear at the club he should have followed his instincts and run.

She was the stuff that S&M porn was made of, and he knew there had to be a catch. He had assumed in the back of his mind that she would ask him for money at the end of the night. He never dreamed it would end up like this.

It was too late to run now, he mused. The clink of his watch against rusted metal resounded in the darkness and he shivered. He suspected he might be the only person left on earth who still wore a wristwatch. He had always been behind the times, and he cursed himself both for a bad pun and for not making the leap into the technology age like everyone else. If he had made that jump, he would have had a cell phone, but he suspected carriers would have zero signal wherever he was. He could at least make light with the phone, and there would have been games to play before he was killed, he thought bitterly. It would also give him something else to think about instead of the constant screaming terror in his head.

He stared around himself. It was dark. He supposed he must have passed out on the way to wherever this place was, since he had no memory of arriving there or of being locked in what seemed to be a rusty cage. He could smell a mix of salt and river water with a hint of wet stone. Underneath it all there was something else lingering in the cold dampness of the stale air. Something that smelled like old roadkill in the last stages of rot.

He pushed the thought out of his head quickly and listened to the darkness in the hope that some sound would offer a clue as to his location. Distantly there came the echo of dripping water on stone. Water always dripped on stone, he thought, and there were always rusty cages in dungeons. He shook his head to clear it of negativity. He strained to hear into the darkness. Far away he heard a ship's horn and his eyes widened with surprise. He was close to the river, possibly just under the river, surely still in the New York City metro area. He must be in one of the old subway tunnels. As if to confirm his idea the cavern began to shake as one of the trains rumbled through high above him. He ducked out of the way of the debris that was shaken loose by the passing train and let out a shaking sigh of relief, clinging to the sounds of civilization.

This had to be some game being played, he was sure of it. The woman from last night was just messing around with him. He frowned. Something about that woman…. She had been familiar, but he could not remember where he had seen her. He leaned against the cold jagged metal of the cage bars and had vague passing thoughts of needing a tetanus shot when he escaped from his prison.

He was drawn out of his musings by a low, almost inaudible sound emanating from the blacker darkness to his right. The sound made the hair on his body stand on end. It did not resemble any sound that he had ever heard in his life. There was water over there, not just a puddle, but deep water from the sound of it. He could hear something large climbing out of the water, its body slapping onto the bedrock floor. It let out a low bellow that seemed almost subsonic then paused.

Tears trickled down his cheeks and he tasted blood where his teeth had sunk into his lips as he bit back a scream of sheer terror. Something about the sound told him that this was not a sex game. This, whatever it was, was for real.

The sounds came again, this time with the added noise of something long slithering free from the depths of the water. He held his breath, waiting. The slithering stopped but was replaced by the sound of bones breaking and resetting themselves. A pained growl echoed around him, amplified by the natural acoustics of the cavern.

He strained to hear the noises of civilization again, any noise other than the animalistic growls in the darkness. A new smell permeated the air and he gagged. Whatever this thing was, it gave off a stench of rotting meat and high tide. The thing turned its head with an audible rush of wind at the noise of his suppressed sickness. He could feel its eyes on him as it began to sniff the air loudly, then it let out a horrible gurgling laugh.

He clasped his hands over his mouth and struggled to breathe as silently as possible, even though he was sure the thing knew he was there and trapped. He heard a slick shuffling in the darkness as the thing made its way around his cage. The sound of its sniffing was like a cough through a segment of PVC piping. As it got closer to one side of the cage, he crawled to the opposite side, trembling with fear.

Something tampered with the lock briefly before sliding away again and he fumbled towards the middle of the cage. His eyes were wide, staring desperately into the blackness as if staring hard enough would let him see what was going on around him. Finally, the thing spoke.

"Where is she?"

The voice was a rough whisper, a ghost from a watery grave. It spoke in a language he had not spoken in millennia, and his heart leapt into his throat as he began to pray.

"No—none of that," the thing hissed, "Who are you that He would bother to listen? You are damned as we all are."

It walked around the cage, circling through the darkness. He felt sure it could see him, despite the lack of light.

"Where is she who brought you here?"

He began to cry with fear, unable to form anything near to coherent in any thought or language. His hands felt through damp straw as he crawled away from the horrible voice and the thing that spoke with that voice. The bars were set wide enough that whatever the thing was out there, it would not be able to reach him until the woman brought the key to unlock the cage.

The putrid smell of the thing grew stronger as it closed in on his prison. It began to rattle the bars, pulling at the door with such force that it moved the entire cage several feet before letting out a hungry, frustrated howl.

He curled into a tight ball in the middle of the cage. It took every ounce of will to stifle his terrified cries.

Something slipped through the bars and slithered toward him. He pulled his foot back with a shout of revulsion and fear. Something slimy and cold had touched him, seeking a hold on his ankle. The smell was unbearable. He gave a short dry heave and heard the thing in the darkness smile. It was the sound of wet lips over sharp teeth.

"She is here."

From out of the darkness beyond the cavern came the quick clack-clack of stiletto boots. The sound approached them from what sounded like a tunnel leading off the main cavern. There was the sound of a heavy door being unlocked, opened, slammed shut, and re-locked from the inside. His heart sank. His prayer had been useless and unheard.

Perhaps it was his own fault, he thought forlornly. He had fallen from grace so gradually over the years that he had barely noticed the downward slide until this moment, when he was faced with his own mortality.

The clack of heels grew louder, and he turned to face the sound. A small flickering light began to illuminate the darkness at the far end of the cavern, drawing closer.

As the light grew brighter the thing that had been trying to tear apart the cage withdrew into the shadows. As it retreated he caught a glimpse of a tentacle that seemed to shrink into a waterlogged hand. The flesh of the hand was gray and shriveled, and the hand pulled away from the light as if in pain.

"You're awake," said a reverberatingly female voice. "I thought you were all about that not dead but dreaming shit."

"Not dead. Not dreaming…. Waiting. By what were you delayed?"

"I had other things to attend to in order to distract the power that is from our little dinner party here."

His breath caught as she came into view. She was beautiful in a way that dragons were beautiful. She was lust in latex, but she was also familiar. She stared down into the cage at him, her long blonde hair a swinging iron curtain behind her and her eyes full of all the warmth of a frozen tundra. The ice of her eyes was not warmed by the sadistic twist of her blood red smile.

"Lilith," he whispered fearfully.

He wondered how he had not recognized her the night before. He had been drunk, true, and possibly drugged, but it had become a coping mechanism over the years for those he had been unable to save in the past. Over the years he had kept clear of Lilith and her kind to avoid their revenge. Last night he had foolishly believed that enough time had passed that none of the remaining Nephilim would remember him or recognize him. He realized now that he was wrong.

"Hello, Enoch."

"I tried to help," he stammered.

"It's not ME you have to explain things to," Lilith smiled coldly, "I wasn't drowned in the flood."

His eyes widened impossibly and he shook his head, the word almost an afterthought. "No…."

She nodded and motioned her head toward the darkness. A pair of glowing eyes glared with hatred at him. Tentacles slithered over the ground, curling angrily before retreating into darkness.

Enoch struggled to speak, but he was frozen with fear. A freakishly tall, naked man walked shakily into the light. He moved as if he were used to walking on the deck of a ship in rough weather. His mouth yawned wide, impossibly wide, showing row upon row of sharp teeth. As he became more fully illuminated the maw shrank and folded into a semblance of a human mouth. The man's sneering smile showed that the teeth were all still there, waiting. Arms and legs relocated into something more human and less tentacle in appearance as he approached the cage again.

The large, watery black eyes stared fishlike and unblinking at Enoch. He could see his own terrified reflection staring back at him from the sunken depths of those horrible orbs.

The man's head was bald and abnormally shaped. The skin was as gray as the shriveled hands and clammy in appearance, as if it had been made of frog skin. The ears were dilating and contracting holes in the side of the man's head. They seemed to breathe in the sounds and regulate them according to loudness. The man's body looked like that of a drowned corpse and there was no doubt of who he was… he was definitely not a man.

Enoch opened and closed his mouth, struggling to breathe and to speak in his guilty defense as Lilith smirked at him and unlocked the cage. She reached into the cage and grabbed him by his collar, dragging him out and dropping him at the feet of the amphibious man.

He climbed to his knees, begging silently, his mouth still refusing to work. The man stared down at him with hate shining in his aqueous eyes. Enoch realized they were squid's eyes and felt his heart gripped in fear. The stories had been true. The flood had not killed them after all.

"Cthulhu," Enoch finally managed to gasp.

He looked up and the man was changing once again, back into his true form that had been hidden by shadows previously. The man's limbs extended and he became larger, the limbs unfurling like lengths of rope. The eyes became like planets, dark matter seeming to swirl in the oil slick depths.

Enoch felt a pain in his chest, a tightening thud as if someone had kicked him in the sternum, and he sat back onto his heels, gasping for air. He looked up at his captors with tears in his eyes.

"Why?" he gasped, trying to focus through the growing pain in his chest.

"It's time," Lilith answered simply.

Her voice sounded far away to his ears and Enoch clutched at his shirt, tearing it open as if it would allow him to get more air into his lungs. To his dismay, there was a tentacle gripping his torso and chest, compressing his ribcage. The tentacle contracted and pushed the air from Enoch's gasping mouth.

Lilith stared up at Enoch as the tentacle lifted him upward, bringing him eye level with a thing that was an abomination in any species. Some of the Nephilim had not turned out quite as pretty as the gods of Olympus. Some had ended up as Cthulhu and Grendel. Some had been subdued by the Great Flood, but not killed by it. That had been Enoch's doing. He had asked the Creator for mercy on behalf of the children of the Watchers, and in the end the Creator had left the drowned Nephilim beneath the ocean, not dead and not alive. Hibernating. Waiting, as Cthulhu had put it only minutes ago.

"Don't feel bad," Lilith told him calmly, as if he were not about to be swallowed whole by a monster, "You're just the first of many. Your part in his death just sweetens the deal."

She shrugged as if to show just how logical and not personal this whole situation was. When she smiled it was a real smile.

"I have to admit, I never expected to see you again. I was surprised to see you at the club of all places, and even more surprised when you didn't recognize me. Imagine how thrilled I was to be able to call up old C-note here and tell him who I had in the cage for dinner tonight!"

"Not my fault," Enoch gasped.

White flowers bloomed in front of his vision and the pain in his chest was getting worse. He almost had to laugh at the irony of having lived so long only to be killed by a heart attack. Then he looked at Cthulhu and his situation lost its irony quickly. He hoped the heart attack took him before Cthulhu did.

"Of what are you speaking?" the monster asked.

The tentacle loosened so that Enoch could breath again. He gasped in grateful gulps of air, though it did nothing to ease the pain in his chest.

"The Flood. It wasn't my fault. I tried to beg for mercy for all Nephilim."

Lilith glanced skeptically at Cthulhu. The monster stared at Enoch for a moment.

"You lie."

"No! I don't lie. You would be dead if I hadn't intervened."

There was silence for a moment as all present paused to consider this statement. The cavern began to rumble and vibrate as a subway rattled through a tunnel closer to them. Larger segments of the ceiling crashed to the floor as the growl of the train moved past.

As soon as the train had passed, Cthulhu turned his attention back to Enoch. "Why should I believe you?"

Enoch was desperate. "Ask Lilith! She can tell you, I don't lie!"

Lilith sat on top of the cage, picking dirt – or possibly dried blood—out from under her fingernails. With a sigh she ignored the statement. Cthulhu looked at her.

"Is it true, Lilith?" the monster gurgled.

"Oh, shit. Yes, okay? It's true. It's all true. Now the big bad truth comes out. Enoch's one of the good guys. He is about as outrageously vanilla as they come. He thinks using coupons at the grocery store is stealing for Christ's sake."

Cthulhu gave a look of confusion at her last statement and his tentacles seemed to shrug. He looked back to Enoch, who was staring with wide terrified eyes at his open mouth.

"I suppose I owe you some thanks, then, Enoch."

Enoch visibly relaxed and gave a short laugh and a relieved wave of his hand.

"Don't mention it, my pleasure."

"I am still very hungry, however."

Enoch's face paled and he started to stare at the gaping maw again. "Maybe we could go out for dinner? Grab a burger and fries? Slice of pizza?" he tried weakly.

Cthulhu shook his massive head and tightened his grip on Enoch. "My apologies, Enoch. You are a good man."

Enoch stared at the row after row of razor teeth stretching before him. His attempts to escape only made Cthulhu grip him harder, and then he had an idea. He struggled harder, hoping he was right. As he had guessed, Cthulhu gripped him more tightly, cutting off his air supply entirely. As the monster lifted him closer to his mouth, Enoch saw black spots covering his vision and felt his consciousness mercifully fade into the darkness.

Cthulhu paused when Enoch went limp in his tentacle. He hated to admit it, but he had spent to much time playing with his dinner instead of just eating. Now it was cold. He let out a great heaving sigh.

"What's wrong?" Lilith asked him.

He motioned toward Enoch's lifeless body slumped in the grip of one large tentacle. Lilith gave a snort of surprise.

"Shit, you killed him." After a pause and a few more feet of slyly calculated distance between her and Cthulhu she asked, "So what are you going to do with him?"

Cthulhu looked at her as if she was an idiot.

"Eat him, of course. That was the plan from the beginning, was it not?"

DEAD GODS DREAMING

By Suzi M

Rhamnous, Attica - Greece, 146 B.C.

The air was heavy with the scent of incense, blood, and fear. Screams of terror rose to the highest summit of the hilltop, reaching deep within the crevasses of the rock formations extending into the rise. The cries came closer, the panic evident in the voices.

In the darkness, eyes opened and stared. Limbs stretched and bodies rose hurriedly to bare feet.

He pulled himself from slumber and sighed, hesitant to leave his dreams and the woman within them. If he concentrated, he could still see her eyes staring into his very soul. Or what was left of his soul, anyway.

He got to his feet and stared toward the dim light of the setting sun filtering through the cracks in the hillside. The cries were just outside the rock formation now, very close. He could hear the group around him waiting hungrily for his command.

"It is time," he said with a grim smile.

His words were echoed on the lips of the gathered women in the darkness of the cavern around them. He could hear the silky rustle of their robes as they moved toward the mouth and toward daylight.

As he exited the mouth of the cave he held a hand up to shield his eyes from the remnants of daylight. The burn in his retinas did nothing to improve his mood and he glared at the group of men and women before him.

"What do you want with us?" he asked the nearest man.

"Please," the man begged, "forgive our intrusion. I must ask for mercy. I have wronged another...," the man's voice trailed off as his eyes rose to meet those of the man at the mouth of the cave.

The man's eyes blazed an unearthly green as he stared at his supplicant. "And?"

"And... and I have come to beg forgiveness. I have brought my youngest daughter for you.... She is a virgin," the man finished.

"What could you have done to this other that requires such a... heavy sacrifice?" the man's deep voice drifted across the hilltop and the crowd fell instantly silent.

The villager fought his growing panic, the explanation caught in his throat. "I ruined a rival merchant," he finally was able to say, "I spread vicious lies to ensure that he would never prosper."

"And as penance your entire village has accompanied you?"

"We were accomplices," whispered another member of the gathered, "We knew he lied, and laughed with him as he boasted of his endeavors."

The man at the mouth of the cave nodded gravely. "The sacrifice then. To atone."

The villager wiped tears from his eyes and stared at the ground, anywhere but at the mouth of the cave or at the group of his accomplices surrounding him. A young girl no more than sixteen was dragged by a small group of people up the mountainside. She struggled and spat, cursing all who held her. When she saw the looming figure at the mouth of the cave she fell silent.

Her eyes were wide as she stared up at him, too afraid to struggle. He was vengeful, filled with wrath. She was merely a small token compared to what he would have done to the people of the village had they not made her their sacrifice.

The people held the girl down on a stone slab as he approached the gathering. The girl screamed and struggled wildly against the hands that held her as he drew near. She begged incoherently to be released, cried out for her father and mother, but they hid their faces in shame and despair.

The man leaned over the slab, breathing in her terror as he traced a slender white index finger over her cheek, following the trail of her tears. He licked his finger, tasting her and his brow furrowed. There was something else beneath her fear. He brought his nose close to the girl's breasts, following the scent first down, then back up to her throat, then to her gasping mouth. He breathed deeply and stared into the girl's eyes. Again he leaned over her and sucked air through his mouth, across his tongue, tasting her. Finally he stood.

He turned slowly, his glare darkening as he frowned at the man who had come to beg his forgiveness and at the other gathered villagers. He was insulted by their lack of devotion. He looked to the group holding the girl and saw the guilt beneath the fear in their eyes.

"This is no virgin," he told them.

The man paled and began to tremble, backing away. He held his hands out before him in a supplicating gesture, as if it could stop what was about to happen.

"Nemesis, I beg you, forgive us," the man tried, "we didn't know!"

Without turning from the slowly retreating group of mortals, Nemesis said over his shoulder, "Ladies… we have work to do."

The faces paled as Nemesis and his Furies advanced, and the girl's screams began afresh. This time her screams were joined by the cries of those who had meant to sacrifice her.

ANGELS FROM THE ASHES OF A HUMAN FIRE

By Suzi M

It was bound to happen sooner or later. It was, after all, inevitable. Like a victim in a bad horror flick I reached out.

My subconscious mind was screaming "Don't do it, you crazy shit! Don't open that door! Stop! Lock that deadbolt again! What the hell are you thinking? You already know who's there! Don't you remember the last time?!"

My subconscious is the asshole in the theater that refuses to shut up, giving his buddy the play-by-play, even though they are in fact watching the same stupid film while sitting next to each other. It is a film everyone else in the theater ends up wishing they waited for the video to come out instead of wasting their time and money to see it in the theater. A nice night out- a date, couples say optimistically before leaving the house. My conscious mind was that optimistic idiot who believed, wholeheartedly, that THIS time, things might be different, even as the CHUD part of my brain was shouting at the screen.

Even as my hands are throwing back the last lock on my door....

It's really not as bad as I remember it, I tell myself. They really aren't Thing 1 and 2 in human form. I really didn't end up in the emergency room getting my stomach pumped because the pizza had the wrong kind of mushrooms on it. I really wasn't dead for a minute and a half....

And they really don't look so dangerous. The night drips off them in wet mumbles splattering the welcome mat mocking its insincerity. Certainly these two men are nothing as grand as the Hunter S. Thompson-esque adventures I have chalked up to their presence in the past. They seem almost forlorn, standing there on my doorstep. In the rain. They look pretty pathetic, really.

"You moved again, you bitch."

The older, more distinguished of the pair nudges his younger, more punk rock companion and lets out a frustrated noise to accompany his glare. They look older. Hell, they ARE older. We are all older. The revelation is nothing short of miraculous. For some reason I hate myself for allowing the knowledge to slip in between the cracks of my secret denial.

"Forgive Xircon, Suz, it's been a fucking bastard of a trip," says the one and only James Glass.

"Good to see you both," I tell them.

It's not really a lie, I think, wondering if two lies make a truth in social mathematics. And it is good to see them both in a way. It has been a hell of long time. Years, actually.

I step aside so they can enter and I take their coats like a good Suzi Homemaker. I am still not sure when the transition from velvet vampiric goth to yoga pants and worn, ripped concert t-shirts happened, but time has a funny way of sneaking up on us all. I bring out towels and some hot coffee for my guests and offer them a seat on the couch. I try not to think about the inevitable stains that will be left on the faux suede.

We stare at each other for a few moments. Or rather, Jim and I stare at each other. Xircon is still sulking and refuses to look at me.

"Sooo…. Took Amtrak?" I try.

Jim looks a little taken aback, as if the thought had never occurred to him to just take the train out into the middle of Pennsylvania.

"We… drove," he says shakily, following his statement up with a little shiver.

"Oh."

There is one thing I am not sure of, and in spite of myself, the lack of knowledge makes me uneasy.

"How in Gods' name did you two find me?"

Xircon glares up and into my eyes finally, growling out, "It wasn't easy. And it cost a hell of a lot."

"Cost?" I ask.

"We…," Jim's mouth opened and closed for a moment or two. He cleared his throat and tried again while smoothing back his wet hair, "We may have filed a missing persons report with Philly's finest."

"You WHAT?!"

I was wrong to believe this could go well, I scold myself. The asshole in the theater part of my brain cackles out an I-told-you-so while flinging popcorn all over the place. I can feel my cheeks draining of blood.

"Oh calm down," Xircon tsks at me, "They just gave us your forwarding address and called us idiots."

James nodded sheepishly at this.

"But I've moved since then, to…. To here."

Xircon nods. "Yeah, it wasn't easy. Good thing your photos are up on MySpace or we'd have never had anything to show around town."

"Everyone's so friendly and helpful out here," James says in something bordering on awe.

"You've been showing my picture around town?" I ask incredulously.

Xircon's smirk says it all. They have been harassing people.

"Out."

"But we just came all this way…"

"Out!"

It goes without saying that I was not expecting them to blink up at me the next morning from the doorstep.

After discovering Xircon and James Glass sleeping on my doorstep, it was with great trepidation that I accepted the offer to go to breakfast with them. My feelings of angst were not because I was afraid of them, but because I have never liked breakfast. The fact that I was awake and on my way to the local diner while the sun was shining was a major negative in my book.

Xircon's driving was another negative in a class all its own. How they made it to my house at all was amazing to me, never mind how we got to the diner. The bumper sticker on the old beatermobile would have been enough to get us shot at, reading 'Give head if you got it!' I got the Combichrist song reference but doubted that anyone else in the area might.

My back was cramping when we pulled into the parking lot of the diner. I climbed out of my hiding space on the floor behind the front seats, and got out of the deathtrap. Both men insisted I wear black and put on some makeup, so I had, and now everyone around us was staring.

We poured into the diner like rock stars, Jim and I having taken a nip or two of Jack Daniel's on the way to the diner and playing keep-away with the flask so Xircon would be unable to drink and drive. Being sober did not sit well with X, and he growled at anyone brave enough to stare at us. He needed a shot of Jack like most people needed a cup of coffee in the morning.

We got seated easily, much to my surprise, and the waitress

seemed genuinely happy to see fellow Goth types. She pointed to my ankh choker and squealed with delight.

"I LOVE your necklace! What kind of cross is that?"

"It's not a cross, it's an ANKH. Can we get some coffee or are there any other elements of her outfit that are shiny enough to catch your attention?" Xircon growled out at the poor kid.

I gave him a hard, steel-toed kick under the table and he let out a cry of pain and surprise. I smiled apologetically at our waitress.

"He's a dick about daytime, and has a newsstand's worth of issues to peruse, but we keep him around because he's so darn pretty."

She smiled amusement at the dig and flipped her notepad to the next available page. Looking to me, she asked, "What can I get you?"

"Coffee, lots of creamers, and some extra sugar."

She gave a quick nod and scanned over Xircon to Jim. "And for you, sir?"

"Coffee as well, and some toast with jam, please," replied the ever-polite Glass-man.

Xircon cleared his throat when the girl turned away from the table. She turned back toward us and faced him with a thin smile, raising an inquisitive eyebrow.

"Aren't you going to ask me what I want?" he sulked.

"Honestly, sir, I don't care what you want," our waitress said in her perky waitress voice, her voice low and the smile frozen to her lips as if she were a ventriloquist that lost her dummy, "It's a shitty job that I hate, and there's not much else I can do around here, so I'm kind of stuck. Then I get to deal with assholes like you on a daily basis. Once if I'm lucky. And you never fucking tip, you cheap bastards. You give the most shit and you never tip. So you see, sir, that what you want is not cost effective, and therefore I will not ask you for what you want, because there's nothing in it for me."

She took a shaking breath and her sunny smile returned as she looked to me and Jim. "My name's Annie, let me know if you need anything. I'll be right back with your drinks."

We sat in silence as our waitress made her way across the restaurant towards the kitchen. Jim and I looked to our companion. Storm clouds could not have looked darker than our friend did at that moment.

"What the fuck are you smiling about?" Xircon growled at me

I blinked, not having realized I was indeed grinning like a maniac. I shrugged, trying to make the smile go away. I could see from Jim's expression that he was fighting his own laughter, but there was more beneath the mirth. There was fear beneath the smile. My own mirth faltered.

"I used to be a waitress, back in the day," I said in way of semi-apology, "and I always wanted to say that to someone who gave me problems."

"It's her job to deal with people like me," Xircon snarled, bringing his fist down onto the tabletop. The jams and various condiments jumped as if frightened.

"Doesn't mean you have to be a dick," I told him.

He glared not at me, but through me. Suddenly I understood Jim's fear. He was scared of Xircon. The look on X's face made the hairs on the back of my neck stand up.

We sat in silence until our waitress returned. As if sensing a shift in the power struggle to name Xircon as a temporary alpha of our little group she sighed and looked at him.

"Can I get you anything?"

Xircon looked up at her, sizing her up, then nodded silently.

"And what can I get for you?"

Xircon smiled suddenly, all charm and sunshine. Jim's eyes widened and his jaw clenched as his hands grabbed for the utensils wrapped in napkins. I almost laughed when it became apparent he was unsheathing a fork.

"I would like a coffee," Xircon said politely.

"OK," our waitress replied. Her tone dropped into cautious hope that maybe she had been wrong about this customer. "Is that it?"

"No. I would also like to rip off your head and spit down your neck."

As we ran from the diner, I could not help but notice that the fork was still missing from the silverware in Jim's former spot at the booth. Xircon was laughing as we piled back into the car.

"What the fuck is wrong with you?" I yelled at him, smacking him in the back of his head.

It happened fast. So fast it took me a minute to fully understand what was happening. There was a distinct click as Xircon grabbed my hand from over the back of the seat. For a moment the glint of the blade and the feel of cold metal pressed against my wrist did not register.

I started to laugh, thinking this must be a sick joke. One look at the horror on Jim's face choked my laughter and I tried to pull away. The blade sank into my skin and I yelled from a sense of detached pain, with more anger than fear at that moment. The fear would inevitably come later.

Blood welled up from the cut and I thanked whatever fluke of genetics I had that made me a slow bleeder. The cut was not life-threatening, but the blade was still pressed against my skin. There was a persistent noise in the car, the roar of panic and raw fear. I looked from my bleeding wrist to Jim. His mouth moved slowly, the fork raised and ready.

"Xirc! Jesus Christ what are you doing!!!"

"You knew the plan before we came out here," Xircon replied calmly, looking into my face, his eyes never leaving mine.

I had never noticed just how blue Xircon's eyes were until that moment. Like ice. His normally bleached white-blond hair was showing black roots to match his eyebrows, eyelashes, and the stubble on his face. The dark circles beneath his eyes were a work over time. He had not slept the night before, and probably had not slept in quite some time. He had the look of a desperate man with handsome features.

"Xircon, what the hell have you done?" I asked quietly.

The corners of his mouth twitched and a sense of dread filled me. The first drops of blood slipped off my wrist and onto the upholstery of the front seat. The drops of my blood fell loudly against the silence.

"It's not what I've done," he said, "It's what I will do."

I looked at Jim, who shook his head, terrified. The fork was raised, ready to plunge forward, but I knew Jim would not have the balls to actually do the deed when it came down to it. The situation and its deterioration into my own peril had not quite sunk in yet. The pain from the cut was far away and surreal, as if I was feeling a ghost pain.

"Oh Godohgodohgod…. Fuck! This wasn't supposed to happen! I'm sorry, Suz, I didn't realize… shit!"

"Let go of my hand," I said calmly, "We'll go get some coffee back at the house."

"No," Xircon said, "You're not going back. You're coming with us."

"I'm going to a hospital to get stitches," I reasoned.

"Don't have to worry about that," Xircon replied, "You'll feel better when you wake up."

Through the fuzzy haze that had snuck up on my brain, sudden realization hit. I was unable to feel panic or pain because I was more or less ready for surgery. But how?

"The flask," Jim suddenly croaked.

"Just enough for the both of you," Xircon said and released my hand.

I fell into the backseat, my head swimming. The screaming coming from the front seat was barely noticeable and quickly faded into the blackness.

Xircon was standing over me when I woke up, and he was smiling. I tried to focus, but the world was swimming around me.

"Come on back," he told me, gently tapping my face.

"What happened?" I asked as he helped me sit up.

"That's a long story," he dropped to the concrete next to me and shrugged, "but we have some time."

"Time?"

"Yes. Lots of time now. All the time in the world, really."

The first inklings of panic crept up my spine. "How long has it been since you slept, Xirc?"

He stared through me, his eyes sunken and cold as a frozen ocean. A small smile of rapture played across his features. "Since the nightmares started."

"You look like hell, you know."

I could hear the fear trembling in my voice now. Whatever he had put in the flask was wearing off.

The expression on Xircon's face was as unresponsive as the

PC blue screen of death. He spit onto the front of his shirt and wiped at something dried and brown. I struggled to focus and realized he was covered in blood.

"Oh shit… Xirc, where's Jim?"

He smiled at me, the pale lines of his face creased and faded as old parchment. "He's fine. He needed to see my reasons for the plan….. I think he gets it now, I really do."

"What plan?"

"You'll have to wait and see," he mumbled around his shirt. He stuffed it further into his mouth, sucking the blood out of the cloth.

"You're starting to scare me," I told him.

There was no disguising the panic in my voice and an involuntary sob leapt from my lips. I looked around us and realized we were in an old factory. I recognized it as the one that had never quite made it to being the new brewery of the area. The gaping and poorly patched cracks in the brick walls explained partially why it sat empty. The debris from the sagging floor above us explained the rest.

"Scratch that, I'm scared."

An expression of pity filled his eyes with tears and he reached a trembling hand out to touch my face.

"How do you think I feel?"

Jim was not his normally gracious self as he came stumbling out of what had been an old freight elevator. He came out swinging, in fact.

Xircon attempted to prevent Jim from approaching me, and

Jim caught him under the jaw with his right fist. Xircon fell back on his ass, glaring angrily up at his partner in crime turned enemy.

"She needs to know why you're here!" Jim shouted down at Xircon.

Xircon grabbed Jim by the legs as he tried to move past him and the two men scuffled on the floor. It would have been funny under other circumstances.

"NOT TIL TOMORROW!" Xircon bellowed, pinning Jim to the ground.

Jim twisted his head around, searching me out. When he caught sight of me he mouthed one word, and it made perfect sense at the time.

I scrambled to my feet and ran for the place we had obviously come through. I jumped over the broken chains and padlock, throwing my hands out in front of me to hit the metal of the door, shoving with all my weight. Behind me I could hear Xircon let out an angry growl of surprise; then a wet crunch that could only be a fist hitting into someone's mouth.

The door groaned and slid about an inch. I stepped back and threw my weight at it again. The sound of metal on concrete set my teeth on edge and then I was stumbling into the blazing light of afternoon. I threw my hands up to shield my eyes from the glare of the parking lot, blinded by the reflected sun. Hands closed over first my arm, then moved up into my hair, pulling me backward as I tried to move forward toward where I knew the street would be.

When I opened my mouth to scream as a hand clamped down over my lips. I bit down as hard as I could. Xircon swore, then did something I never dreamed he would or could do: he hit me.

"Stupid bitch, I'm trying to save you," he growled as he dragged me back inside the abandoned brewery.

"How the hell are you planning to do that?" I asked, trying to twist away from him.

My face hurt where he had punched me and I wanted so badly to show him the underside of my steel-toes. He was stronger than I had ever given him credit for, and in spite of my usual ability to defend myself, he had desperation and sheer panic on his side. Too quickly I was back on the filthy concrete floor and the door was slammed shut behind us.

Jim groaned from across the empty space, his voice echoing off the exposed metal girders. It became abundantly clear that we were fucked. He pushed himself onto his elbows and then to his knees, breathing hard to lessen the pain of the beating Xircon had given him. He looked at me through swollen eyes, a silent apology.

Xircon picked up a broken length of pipe from near the door, dragging it behind him as he approached us. The sound of metal on concrete was less than reassuring. He lifted his newfound weapon at both me and Jim, pointing, his face contorted with anger and fear.

"If either of you tries to get away again, I swear to Christ, I'll just fucking end it for you. It'll be faster, and you'll thank me."

He fell to the floor, blocking us from the door. The circles around his eyes were darker now, and he stared off into the corner as if someone spoke to him. I looked to Jim and silently pleaded for an explanation. He shook his head at me.

"What the hell is going on here?" I finally asked.

Xircon's detached gaze snapped to mine. The sudden intensity of it, the focus of it, was frightening.

"You're not going to believe me, but I saw Nemesis. He was walking down 6th Avenue. He talked to me."

I blinked at him and Jim covered his face with a groan. It was impossible that he could have seen a character from one of my novels, and odds were good that he had seen someone that resembled Nemesis in New York City. Shit. How many tall, pale Goth men were wandering the city that never slept? We were so fucked.

"Oh? What did he tell you?"

"He…. He said he was coming for you," Xircon's face screwed up in an effort to stay calm, "I don't think he wanted to have milk and cookies. He said to tell you he would find you, and you would know it was really him because death would follow in his wake."

"Well," I breathed. I was unnerved by the eerily accurate words that, had Nemesis been real, he would have spoken. "Did he say when?"

"On the next new moon," Xircon said with a shuttering laugh, "That fucker is so much scarier in person, you know it?"

I nodded cautiously, feeling the blood draining from my face.

"New moon… That's tonight… When did the nightmares start, Xirc?"

"That same night," he said and his words were followed by a sudden sob. "He was in my head, trying to figure out where you were, but I didn't know! When I found you, I stopped sleeping so he wouldn't find out," his words trailed off into horrified babbling and he hugged the pipe to his chest. "You have to kill me," he said.

"NO!" Jim shouted, moving quickly to slap Xircon across the face and end the terrified rambling, "Xircon, she doesn't even believe you, and he's hers! You've completely lost it! Can we please just stop all this now? Please?"

"Shit. He's here," Xircon whispered.

The door flew open behind us, slamming against the bricks hard enough to send debris cascading down the wall. A looming shadow filled the doorway.

"Found you," it said.

SAMEDI

By Suzi M

He used to be something back in his day….

He thought this as he stared into the dregs of his rum, turned the color of weak tea by ice long-melted. The bar was hot as shit, always was. They didn't believe in air conditioning in this section of town. They called it 'ambiance' now and sold it to tourists at $7.50 a shot. Shit, how they got away with things in the name of tourism.

People feared him. Used to fear him, he reminded himself, before Mardi Gras went to Disneyworld on vacation and came back again on a greeting card. Now he was stuck in this shitty bar hiding from Mama Brigitte after their latest argument. He sucked down the remainder of the rum, grinding the last pieces of ice bitterly at the recollection of how he had come to be in his present state. Damn woman.

With an angry tug, he adjusted the ends of his threadbare tux. He took a drag off his cigar and flicked a stray ash from his equally threadbare top hat. He stared bleakly at the empty bar around him. They still feared him, on some unconscious level, and this cheered him. Who gave a shit if they couldn't see him?

Dixieland music was piped through tired old speakers as he smacked his now empty glass onto the graffiti carved bar top. The painted woman behind the bar sauntered over with a look to go with the sour mash in her own glass.

The ice she refilled him with looked about the same color as the rum that followed. Shit, what the hell was he doing here? He winked at the bartender. She stared back with blank eyes, unimpressed.

"Did you hear the one about the man from Venus?" he asked casually.

She grunted, shook her head, and walked back to the other end of the bar. He watched her ass as she went. Nice ass, he thought and felt the grin spread over his face.

"You wanna go fuck?" he yelled down the bar.

"Nah," said the bartender, leaning over a dog-eared book.

"I can pay," he tried, but didn't feel the confidence to go with the words.

"Nah," came the reply.

Shit, he really was having a bad day to be turned down by a whore. He took a swig of his rum and leaned onto the bar, dejected.

The doors banged opened, illuminating the dingy bar with nicotine stained light.

Two girls came stumbling in, giggling and clinging to each other for balance. They were practically weighed down by Mardi Gras beads.

"Ladies," Baron Samedi said and his lewd grin resurfaced.

They stopped laughing and looked him over. The one closest to him was a pretty little thing, with caramel skin and thick, curly black hair that framed equally dark eyes. She reeked of liquor and beer. The girl clinging to her was just as pretty as her friend, with straight blond hair and blue eyes. They stared at him, trying to focus, then burst out in giggles again.

"You have a skull face," the blond girl said with much concentration. Her finger pointed as if he was not aware of his own head.

Her friend seemed to take notice of their surroundings suddenly, glancing back and forth between Samedi and the bartender, and her expression sobered. She dropped her eyes and nudged her drinking buddy.

"Shhh. Let's go. We'll find someplace else to go to the bathroom," she whispered.

"I wanna stay here and talk up Mr. Skullface," the blond laughed and moved as if to sit at the bar, "Mind if I join you there, Skeletor?"

"Not at all," Baron Samedi said with a cold smile.

"We really need to go," the dark-haired one said, dragging her companion back out into the daylight.

He could hear them just outside the door, the blond complaining that her friend was no fun, and the dark-haired one explaining who he was.

"Good thing you din' fuck dem gurls."

Samedi looked up in surprise at the bartender.

"Holy shit, you can talk!"

"Mmmm," she muttered, never raising her eyes from her book.

"I wasn't going to fuck them," he tried.

The bartender gave him a doubtful glance, then returned her eyes to story.

"At least not at the same time."

The bartender snorted into her book.

"Shit," he swore quietly and pushed his glass over for a refill.

It wasn't often he felt like coming over to this side to visit, and now this. He sucked down the rum, finished his cigar and stared hard at the bartender.

"This is a barely agreeable place to visit, and I'm fucking glad I don't live here."

He stood up from his bar stool and remembered what being drunk was all about. When he looked back at the bartender he recognized his wife. She grinned at him.

He returned the grin just before his ass hit the sticky floor of the bar.

FURY

By Suzi M

To say her act was exotic was probably the biggest understatement since someone cut up a loaf of bread and called it the best thing. Her act was the stuff of wet dreams and quickie afternoon sessions of self-abuse. She was the guilty fantasy, the picture in a man's head as he fucked his cow of a wife.

The music began for her set and she walked onto the stage. The ambient noise of conversation and catcalls ended abruptly as she began to dance. Slowly, deliberately, she moved with the music and dropped her semi-fitted dress to the floor without touching it.

Beneath her black lace dress were black latex panties and a black latex bra. A delicate chain of silver encircled her waist, running through the hoop of her navel ring.

The audience stared in rapt attention, some men had forgotten the money they held in their hands. Others had spilled their drinks into their laps.

She tilted the corners of her mouth into a perfect rendition of a knowing smile and reached up toward her head. With a wet lick of her blood-red lips she let her blond hair loose from its bondage, and felt it cascade down her naked back as she turned to face her audience. Her mouth twisted to a perfectly twisted smile, and she regarded every last one of the men beneath her with ice blue eyes as she mounted the pole. She scissored her thighs around it and locked it there, allowing the pole's turn to perpetuate the illusion she was sliding in a horizontal circle.

With a swift flick she released the front of her top from her upside-down position into the breathlessly silent audience. The beat of the music was driving; filled with so much bass she could feel it in her thighs, sex before it became a tumultuous fuckfest.

She wrapped one long leg up the pole, the black latex of her thigh high boot appearing to slither like a snake over the brass. Her other leg she wrapped down the pole, her hands propping her in place more than her legs. With a twist of her body and perfectly on beat, she flipped upside down, her legs twined around the pole as she held her arms out to the audience.

She eased her hold on the pole slightly and slid down until her hands touched the floor. She released from the pole into a handstand, then kicked each leg deliberately one by one to the floor and stood up, continuing to move with the music all the while.

Her sisters were working the crowd, but knew that during her set they would not be needed by any of the patrons. One of the younger sisters came to the stage, where she leaned over until her breasts were all but out of the shiny slick vinyl of her top. She gripped a dollar in her teeth.

"Lilith," she sang quietly, a smile of mischief lighting her face.

Lilith returned the smile and dropped to all fours. She crawled carefully, each movement of her body exaggerated for effect to keep in time with the beat. When she reached the girl with the dollar she took the other end of the bill in her teeth. They danced together, their lips so close and eyes locked. They could swear they heard zippers in several pairs of blue-jeans breaking at that moment.

By the end of her set, Lilith always had a line of men waiting for the second half of her act: when she put her clothes back on and beat the shit out of every last one of them.

As they screamed her name behind the ball-gag she felt only the electric surge of power. They loved her, and she loathed them. They were a means to an end only, passing time until Nemesis returned to lead them once more, to give them purpose.

She gave the bared ass before her a hard hit, breaking the riding crop in the process. The man began to cry in low, miserable sobs. Blood welled up in the wake of the crop, tiny beads at first and then small rivulets. Lilith reached to the table on which she kept her implements of pain, bringing over a bottle of vodka. She poured it onto the man's cuts and he writhed, crying out in renewed pain before finally screaming out the safe word.

She walked around him, faced him, then took his face in her hands. Almost lovingly, she licked away his tears.

The man turned his face away, regretting that he had come to her and knowing he would be back again. He also knew he would once more cry out the safe word and earn her scorn. He hated himself for his own weakness, never suspecting this woman was nowhere near human.

"I will give you advice," she said to the man, "Never fall in love with a Fury."

With almost cruel glee she released him from his bonds and stepped to the doorway. He struggled to re-arrange his clothes and cover himself, but it was the final humiliation. The line of men would laugh when they caught sight of his trembling, half-naked form huddled in the corner. Each believing that he would not be reduced to this man's state, and each finding out how wrong he was by the end. The man ran past Lilith, avoiding eye contact with her and with the others waiting for their turn. Lilith stared at them all, wishing she could kill them. Soon, she promised herself silently.

Out loud she said only, "Next."

This time the screams began before the door had even finished closing.

THE END OF LOVE

By Suzi M

The light swirled in hazy afternoon shafts as it filtered through yellowed panes of glass and onto the bleached Oriental rug. The dust they had kicked up while dancing created motes that played with the dingy illumination, like spotlights after the play was done. Quiet rustling came from their antique hems as they moved across the floor, twirling to the music as it crackled from the old radio. When the music stopped they looked at each other with knowing, sad smiles.

They took a bow, their too-big clothing sagging from their shoulders and their shadow audience already flitting to the darkening corners of the room. Wallpaper hung in tattered ribbons, curling off the plaster in flypaper strips, exposing water stains long dry-rotted on the plaster beneath. It was reminiscent of an ancient clown peeling off its smile.

"One more?" Prometheus whispered.

Pandora shrugged.

They began to dance, this time with no music to accompany their steps. The radio crackled dead air into the stillness and they cast tired eyes toward the center of the room.

A box sat open and empty in the middle of the floor. It was an ancient piece of craftsmanship, with heavy carvings in the lid and sides, built to last. It survived in their care for quite some time, and they had borne their burden quietly.

After millennia of inconspicuous boxiness, the box had started to whisper and hum one day. At first they were afraid, and hid the box in the attic, remembering the last time it had been opened. Days and weeks passed. The whispering and humming had grown louder until finally it filled their nights and days with a sinister dread.

There were no words to describe what had happened when the lid had finally come free in their curious, fearful grasp. Once there had been only hope contained in the box. Hope was a harmless thing, until it was stacked against the latest atrocities man had invented over the years. It had evolved into a hope in hell, and after that there was nothing left.

And now they danced, because history suggested that in the face of tragedy humans were known to occasionally go down gracefully. They had been dancing for days waiting for the time when it was all over. The radio's sudden silence was their proof. The silence stretched between their slowing movements of a dance from ancient Greece. The silence was no disc jockey's accidental hitting of the wrong button, no commercial break gone wrong. Somewhere on the other end of the transmission was a dead deejay.

They continued to dance in the silence because it seemed the right thing to do when the world was coming to an end.

THE FOUR GOLDFISH OF THE APOCALYPSE

By Suzi M

When do you go to die, blessed bowl-dweller? Golden shining in the darkness of a bedroom that never sleeps. Greenery surrounding on all sides like an indoor jungle, swim through the cool calm water and wait. Something is coming.

And you in the brandy snifter, who have never tasted of alcohol, but would breathe it if you could, what say you to war? Surrounded in peace and tranquility in a living room that never dies, swim through the warm sunny water and wait. Something is coming.

Twins, Pisces, in a spare room with no room to spare, how do you feel about the threat of disease and famine, in a world you will never have to see? You will only fear the horrors of Ick, and that perhaps you will only eat once today. You swim in silver, surrounded by songs and the canvases of an unknown artist, watching the smeared image of the outside world. Swim so softly and wait. Something is coming.

Movement in the darkness, and the swipe of furry paw through the dark water, golden fins swished in counter-attack. The next day found Princess missing and presumed innocent. The feline had it coming, every night was another attempt to obtain sushi, and not very fair when the target is trapped in a small glass bowl. So ended the tyranny of the family cat.

Cleaning day, try to swim to safety, end up in a drain trap. Harsh metal an unwelcome change to the silky soft caress of clean water. Air rushing at gasping gills, and no breath to be had. That night the family broke apart in a burst of rage from all sides. Divorce was imminent from the moment of the final battle.

Twin quicksilver rushing at glass walls in an attempt at escape where none is to be had. Pudgy sticky fingers grope to pet and coddle, uncaring of the delicate balance of the pH of the water and the pollution of chocolate and sugar that pours into angry gills. Water clouding with sugar and caffeine, caramel colors, and other artificial ingredients that were never meant to be breathed. That night the scratching of rodents is heard in the attic, and a toddler falls ill. An inspection discovers that the home is infested with rats, and the child has contracted the Plague. It is the first case of the Plague recorded in many decades, and considered a freak occurrence. The rats are also deemed to be the bringers of the Plague. Within a month the eldest daughter is hospitalized with a diagnosis of anorexia nervosa. The cracks in the family widen. Something is coming.

Shouts of anger erupt, shattering the stillness of the night. Objects thrown break on impact and more voices raised in anger. Blame is thrown back and forth, and the final crash brings down the alpha male. A second crash ruptures the skull of the dominant female, and after all, everyone dies.

DREAMING OF ARTAUD

By Suzi M

The air was filled with the scent and crash of the ocean as Artaud began his story. I nodded in all the right places, smiling politely every now and then, and still unsure of how I had ended up on a beach in Egypt walking along the sand with a ranting madman.

"I used to be a story-teller," he says bitterly, almost as if he has read my thoughts of him.

We continue walking, the ocean's roar made more deafening by the darkness of the night. The salt spray clung to me, and I could feel its sting in my lungs. I wondered about this old man on the beach, the tight-lipped edges of his mouth stained by laudanum, and his face made haggard by life instead of by nature.

"I was famous in my time," he explains to me. "They called me Artaud, giving me a god's status until I told the story they didn't want to hear."

Artaud spits on the sand and I remain respectfully silent. Our steps become lost in the waves when we wander too close to the ocean, the silence almost louder than the waves.

"What happened then?" I ask after a small eternity.

"This!" he cries, motioning to all around us. "France wasted away without my words and became a desert on an ocean."

"But we're in Egypt."

His eyes glare into my soul and I shudder, huddling into the warmth of my sweater, my layers of clothing. His lips become tighter when he tells me, "We are in France."

And the subject is closed. I shrug to pretend I'm not afraid, but I can see the points of the pyramids just over the dunes. I can see the outline of the Sphinx in his crazed eyes.

"I have been outcast for many years," Artaud continues as if he had never stopped talking, poking at objects on the beach with a piece of driftwood. "The story I told was a truth that no one wanted to utter. I had hoped to release the society from the shackles of the words no one would say. My efforts earned me ridicule and exile instead."

His face is sullen and he pokes angrily into the hieroglyphic sand. I am hungry and I reach into the churning water to draw out a scallop. When I look up Artaud has moved further down the beach, and I must run to catch up with him.

"I found a better audience than those fools," he says quietly.

I chew absently on the scallop, eating it raw, shell and all. Artaud is annoyed by the crunching noise, but he says nothing about it, only glares over his hunched shoulder at me from time to time.

"I have been writing my stories in the sand for twenty years. Every morning the ocean rises to meet me at its shores so that it may lap up the stories I write, and every evening it returns for the second half of the story. Last week I heard the ocean telling the seagulls the story I had given it only that morning."

Artaud beams at me and at the ocean, and I feel an overwhelming sense of sadness for the man. He looks at me with eyes lit from within by insanity, his hair bleached white by age and the sun, his features lined and chiseled away by tears, wind, and rain.

"Tell me a story," he says suddenly.

I put the last of the scallop into my mouth and chew thoughtfully, wondering what story I could possibly tell a man who had written countless stories to be washed away by the ocean.

"It doesn't have to be anything grand or elaborate," he tells me, "Just something. Anything. I've spent my whole life telling stories to everyone and no one, now I want someone to tell me a story."

I stare out at the crashing waves of the ocean for a moment, so gray and dreary somehow. The wind catches the hem of my skirt, tearing the wet fabric at my ankles and filling me with sand. I look back to Artaud, my eyes stung by tears as I tell him his story.

"Last night I ate shellfish by the ocean, in the company of an old man who told me stories so that I would stay there and keep him from being lonely. He had been exiled to a beautiful beach, with no one to talk to. Before the night-lit beach exile, he had been a teller of stories until one day he had told a story his society didn't want to hear, and they cast him out.

"He had started to write his stories in the sand of the beach, telling the tales to the ocean waves and wet sand, believing that the waves lapped up his words as eager ears would. He was completely insane, and called himself Artaud. He claimed we were in France, but I knew he was wrong. We were in Northern Africa. I knew somehow that if we crossed the dunes we would end up in the desert that he claimed was France without his words.

"Artaud asked me to tell him a story, that he was old and tired and mad from the world, that for once, before he died, he wanted someone to tell him a story. He suggested we walk while I told it, and I ate shellfish shell and all as I talked. I told him my stories, but they weren't my stories. They were the stories of someone else's lifetime. Of a dream. I pointed out the pyramids on the horizon as we walked, and he pretended not to see them, refused to see them, as he still held fast to his belief that we were in France without his words.

"I was sad to leave this strange man, and I promised to visit him again, even though I had no real intention of doing so. He knew that I lied to him, but appreciated the sentiment behind the lie. He wished me a fond farewell, and I never saw him again."

I look at Artaud and he is so pale and small, his body fighting the pull of the cold wind. His old face wrinkles into a sad smile and I conclude my story with the words, "The End."

"Walk with me only a little further," he says and his words are pulled from his lips by the jealous wind and the shrieking waves. He seems to deteriorate as we walk, becoming older, more weather-beaten, falling away one grain of sand at a time.

"I waited so long for you to come to me, on this beach, in this place. It was a place I knew we would be able to speak freely. To be ourselves in a wasteland of no barriers. These few moments alone with you, without the invasion of the world, have been more precious to me than any moments we stole together in life."

We walk further down the beach, and he takes me by the arm, saying that he knew I would be leaving him soon, and thanks me for visiting him. He tells me I am more beautiful than ever, that I still look like the moon-goddess. I ask him what he means, and he only smiles, mouth stained at the edges with the faded markings of laudanum.

THE STONEHENGE MAN INCIDENT

By Suzi M

October 5th, 2012, Excerpt from The Mourning Son Times

Early today the remains of an unidentified man were discovered by tourists in the center of Stonehenge. Cause of death could not immediately be discovered. Upon inspection of the body, a note and newspaper clippings were found. Investigators ask that any person with information as to the man's identity please contact the lead inspector directly.

October 7th, 2012 Excerpt from The Mourning Son Times

Investigators have released more information pertaining to the mystery man found dead two days ago in Stonehenge's center. The note found on the body has been released to the public and reads as follows:

"Sir or Madam,

If you are reading this letter, you have no doubt found my body and I have been successful in my efforts. Please waste no time investigating my cause of death, but focus instead upon the seas.

On [ed. note: date with-held for national security purposes] the oceans will reveal more than we could have dreamed possible and will usher in a new [ed. note: damages to the pages rendered this portion of the letter unreadable] waste no time!

Following the first occurrence described above, more signs will become clear. Be ever-vigilant for those signs.

While the first event occurs at [ed. note: location, date and time with-held due to national security concerns], the second will be much more obvious and take place on [ed. note: location, date and time with-held due to national security concerns].

I have done all I can to deliver this message. I can only hope that it has been delivered in time.

H–"

October 10th, 2012 Excerpt from The Mourning Son Times

Speculation continues as to the identity of the man found in Stonehenge and the meaning behind his mysterious note of apparent warning. The story has become a worldwide puzzle as the online community attempts to decipher his message.

The note and the man's belongings have been examined thoroughly, but no matches on fingerprints have been returned. The man, and his message, remain a mystery, though there are those in authority who suspect the entire affair to be a hoax based on the 2012 Mayan prophesies.

October 15th, 2012 Excerpt from The Mourning Son Times

Late last night an entire population went missing at Belfastershire. The small village is typically a tourist attraction, but sometime between 8pm and 4am all residents and tourists abandoned the quaint seaside destination for parts unknown. Authorities were alerted when a group of teens returning from London discovered their families had disappeared without a trace.

No bodies have been recovered, and there is no evidence of foul play. One investigator who wishes to remain anonymous hypothesized that the entire town's disappearance is merely a publicity stunt to boost tourism.

October 20th, 2012 Excerpt from The Mourning Son Times

Yet another seaside town has vanished during the night. Panic has erupted in the surrounding towns as fear of being the next unintentional migration mounts. Officials continue to assure the populace that all is well.

In a related vein, more pieces of the puzzle of the 'Stonehenge Man' as he has come to be known have been released to the public. Most of the released information is basic, from the type of clothing he wore to the color of his hair. Other, unofficial, sources have leaked that the newspaper clippings found on his person were from this very newspaper, but of articles that had not yet been written or published.

October 30th, 2012 Excerpt from The Mourning Son Times

Following riots in London and mass exodus from seaside towns to safer inland habitations, officials have finally released the strange Stonehenge Man newspaper clippings to the public. Only one remained that had not yet occurred at the time of this writing. It is printed below:

"October 31st, 2012 The Mourning Son Times Evening Edition

Earlier this afternoon the mystery of the missing seaside towns was solved, but not before all seaside town populations were destroyed by what appeared to be [ed. note: damage to the newspaper clipping rendered this segment unreadable]. At around 1pm, all residents in every coastal town were found dead, the trail of carnage spreading inland. The murders are thought to be a result of [ed. note: damage to clipping has rendered this portion unreadable].

It is strongly advised that all citizens remain calm while evacuation measures are implemented.

[ed. note: a tear in the clipping removed the remaining article contents.]

October 31st, 2012 Excerpt from The Mourning Son Evening Edition

Earlier this afternoon the mystery of the missing seaside towns was solved, but not before all seaside town populations were destroyed by what appeared to a terrified mob of locals in each town. At around 1pm, all residents in every coastal town were found dead, the trail of carnage spreading inland. The murders are thought to be a result of the initial and unauthorized printing of the October 31st evening edition partial excerpt from a clipping retrieved from the body of the Stonehenge Man.

Until the mobs can be brought under control, evacuation seems to be the only solution.

It is strongly advised that all citizens remain calm while evacuation measures are implemented.

The editors and staff at The Mourning Son Times sincerely apologize for having used our media outlet for the propagation of lies. The story of the Stonehenge Man was meant to be a Halloween prank only and was never meant to become a worldwide phenomena.

Again, we are truly sorry and hope that the survivors of our unintentional catastrophe remain safe. May God have mercy on us all.

BEAUTIFUL DOLL

By Suzi M

The televisions in the bar were all tuned to various news reports about revolution and murder. Assassinations, parties and purgatories seemed to be all the rage. He took the last swig of his whiskey and slammed the rocks glass on the scarred bar top, signaling to the bartender that he would like another double served up straight.

"Hell of a night," the bartender said in the emotional yet flat tone that bartenders reserved for the interloper patrons.

"You have no idea."

The bartender made a quick show of topping off the rocks glass, giving an extra splash to bring the amber liquid to the rim. He pulled a ten dollar bill across the bar and moved to make change.

The general hush of the bar was broken when someone pushed bills into the jukebox and started tapping on songs to play.

He was shocked to hear a song from the 40's. He turned to look at the bar patron that had played such an old song.

She was the stuff of Noir detective novels. He could not be sure, but she seemed to gain color as she stood there, as if she had been a black and white photograph come to life.

Her heels clacked solidly across the bar floor as Al Jolson belted out a song that in modern times would have earned him a serious restraining order. Such was the way of romance, he supposed. Come closer, come closer, come closer -- too close.

She smirked and her dark gray lips turned cherry red in the warm glow of the bar lights. Her gray suit was still gray, but her gray flesh and hair warmed to a healthy glow. Gray eyes twinkled to blue as she sat down next to him. She removed her hat and gloves, arranging them neatly on the seat beside her.

He watched her out of the corner of his eye, pretending to be intensely interested in the whiskey he clutched in his hand. He could feel her glance as it slid over him before she waved to catch the bartender's attention.

"What can I get you, doll?" the big man asked.

"I would like a martini, please," she said quietly.

"Sure, hon, what kind?"

She stared at the bartender blankly.

"Chocolate, vodka, you know… what kind? Just regular?"

"Yes, just a regular martini, thanks."

He struggled to place her accent. It sounded familiar and yet foreign. Local women sure as hell didn't talk the way this dame did.

"I got it," he told the bartender when he returned with the drink and the woman began to open her purse.

The bartender nodded and walked away, leaving the drink behind. The woman smiled shyly, glancing at him from the corner of her eye. Not quite looking at him, but somehow he felt as if she was staring straight into his eyes.

"Thank you, mister...."

He waved a dismissive hand. "Don't mention it. You played my favorite song."

She looked perplexed for a moment, listening. "I didn't play this song," she finally said.

"Doesn't much matter," he shrugged, "To good timing," he continued, raising his glass.

"Indeed," she said and raised her own glass.

After a heavy pause he said, "So what's your story?" his eyes stared straight ahead, as if he were talking to the shelves of bottles instead of one of the most gorgeous women he had ever seen.

"My story?" she asked the liquor bottles.

"How'd you end up here?"

"I'm not sure I know what you mean," she said, her smile communicating polite confusion.

"We all have a story," he told her, then pointed to the bartender, "See Ken over there? He ended up here after his wife left him."

"Oh, how sad for him," she said quietly and took a shaking sip of her drink.

"And Charlie over there," he said, pointing to a bedraggled man in a wilted clown costume, "He fell off the wagon. Never went back to the circus."

"This is *not* how it's played," she said suddenly.

"Well, you wanted me to play."

"Yeah, but you're supposed to be the *detective*, and you're supposed to figure out my history."

"And since you're going to tell me anyway… who are you supposed to be in this game?"

She let out a frustrated sigh. "I'm the femme fatale."

He slammed against the bar suddenly as if giant hands had dropped him, which they had. He watched his drink slide and fall over the side of the bar top, unable to save it without blowing his cover.

"I don't even know what a fem-fatal is, so how am I going to figure out your stupid doll's history?"

"Femme fataaall," she corrected.

The voices faded, still arguing, and he slumped. The bartender stared blue-eyed and plastic at an odd angle, as if listening to something no one else could hear. He wore an idiot's grin.

He glanced at his companion and was dismayed to see that she held the same smiling lifelessness as the bartender. When he picked up her drink from her stiffened hand, he sighed with disappointment. The martini glass was filled with clear resin and plastic olives.

"Seamus," he told the blonde, "my name is Seamus. See you next time the kids decide to play Maltese Falcon."

He put on his hat and trench coat, frowning at the dolls surrounding him in the play bar. He shook his head and smirked, then. At least those damned kids had not gotten his gold.

THE DEMON'S TALE (Expanded Edition)

By Suzi M

"In order to fight evil, you must first know what evil is."

Its silver eyes are unblinking, focused upon me. First, let it be known that I did not summon this demon. Also let it be known that I am repentant for the wrongs I have committed, should I die here tonight. I ask its name and it smiles.

"Norad."

"Norad?"

Its grin widens to show broken teeth. "Yes. I like Norad."

"Very well. Norad."

Its gaze is filled with the madness of the damned, and I ask God in His mercy to give me the strength to escape this creature. A cry escapes me as its clawed hand runs up my arm. I begin to pray, clutching my rosary, focusing on the tenets.

"Apologies," it says, "Your kind are so... untainted. I could not help myself. I needed to make sure you were really here."

The demon's silver eyes lock with mine and I fight the urge to run from it. The demon has made it clear that I cannot run. It leans closer to me and I can smell the brimstone upon its gray skin. My fingers move to the next bead and in my head I say a silent 'Hail Mary'.

"There are those of my kind that would break you," it tells me, its voice a harsh rasp in the darkness.

"And you will not?"

It stares again, silver distance in its eyes. Finally it shakes its head.

"No... we cannot harm you."

"We?"

"My kind. We have sworn."

Norad settles back as if the answer is satisfactory for all further inquiry. All the demon has done is left me with so many more questions.

There were 30 of us when we entered the tunnels. We were fools to have gone against the mandate of the Bishop and fools to have ignored our own fears! I do not know where my brothers of the cloth are, or if they are yet alive....

For years - decades, possibly even centuries - we had been both forbidden and afraid to venture into the darkened spaces beneath the Tor. Despite the churches we had built to suppress the pagan elements of the area, we held to an unspoken dread of the horrors just out of our sight in the passages we had discovered under our church.

When I was a much younger man and still but a novice I once stepped into those recesses. Few steps had I gone when the noises began. Old fables of the underworld and the Faery King rose to meet my footfalls and I fled back into the light. In my lifetime only one man had dared to venture further into the tunnels. He never returned.

When I and 29 of my brothers made the decision to explore the darkness to reclaim the space as catacombs it was a decision borne of sacramental wine and bravado. A somber silence befell us not ten yards into the tunnels... and then began the shouts of fear followed by utter darkness.

The demon's words rouse me from my morbid thoughts. "You must remember this meeting," it tells me, "and you must record my words for future generations."

"I shall do no such thing!"

"You will," the demon hisses, "You MUST. It is for the good of the world."

"What care you for good? Demons are known to deceive."

Norad sighs heavily and sinks to the floor. "There were 30 of you."

"Yes."

"Three of you will emerge on the other side."

"How can you know that? What will happen to the others?"

"THREE emerge," the demon repeats, "That is all I know."

"What happens to –"

"Dammit, man, it is all history has told us! I am here to tell one of the three to end the madness before it begins!"

"How do you know that I am the one to tell?"

The demon stares at me, through me. I feel a shiver run over my spine.

"I don't. If I fail tonight I will have to return again until it works."

A sudden wrenching sensation seizes my insides. The thought in my mind I dread to voice aloud.

"Have there been others before me?"

The demon nods.

"How many?"

"Two."

"I am the last of the three?"

Again, the demon nods.

"You said that you would need to return again... If I am the last.... What has happened to the others?"

The demon glares at me, its unholy eyes burning into my very soul.

"We have been through this before, you and I. And I will return until you listen and understand what I am saying, nevermind the others."

***

The demon paces before me, its body emanating a gray aura as it walks through light and shadow. Its gaze occasionally turns toward me and I can feel its anger and frustration that it has not yet acquired my soul. The rage emanates from it like the heat of hellfire.

"It's similar to the purgatory your kind have preached for centuries," it says suddenly, "Each time I return to this place, to this same conversation. Each time I try to make the outcome different than the time before it, and each time it's always the same."

"That is because your kind have no free will," I tell the miserable creature and feel a swell of pride in my humanity.

The demon sighs. "You have grasped nothing of what I have told you, have you?"

I return its contempt in my gaze, allowing silence to stretch between us in answer.

"Let's go over this *one… more… time….*I am here to *help.* The world is in danger and humanity is close to extinction.

"We've traced the source of many problems back to this era, to the religious figures of the time. The various battles that have been fought in the name of God, the lands explored and taken in the name of religious freedom have all culminated in a world filled with war, greed, and famine."

It stares at me, expecting something. I frown at it.

"You lie, demon. It is in your nature to lie, and this is just one of many you will tell me tonight in the hopes that you can bend the future to evil."

The thing called Norad lets its mouth fall open in shock. It is clear that I have seen through its lies. It lets out a brief bark of laughter and falls back against the wall.

"I will tell you a story of the future," it says after a pause, "and if you are still unconvinced, then…. Perhaps the future deserves to die."

It takes a long breath then closes its eyes for a moment before beginning its tale.

"The Industrial Revolution changed the world. The population exploded, people began to live longer, and corporations were born. The shift took decades, but it happened. Government became so convoluted that the true wielders of power were not the men in charge, but the secret underlings.

"Written laws became so filled with extraneous and vague wording that the laws lost all meaning or were interpreted in such a way that no one could truly argue the legality. Companies made profits and killed the world in their wake. Some pharmaceutical companies went so far as to dispose of their medicine in water that would later be consumed by citizens, claiming it would not affect those who drank it because there was not enough of the medication to be considered tampering with the water supply.

"Meanwhile a much darker thing was occurring. Governments were encouraging this drugging of the masses, and the wealthiest of families prepared for the worst-case scenario while staying safely out of harm's way. During the mid 20th century the government of one of the most powerful nations on earth began to test mind control techniques on innocent subjects. Shortly after the official statement that the covert experiments were no longer being carried out, a series of proposals came through various branches of the same government suggesting that fake attacks be committed against the citizens in the name of an enemy state in order to justify a war.

"Food became pre-packaged and over-processed swill that was so full of preservatives and fat that people were becoming obese over the years while still lacking basic nutrition. Little by little the entire population of the nation grew lazy, complacent, and lacking enough motivation to fight for basic survival. Subliminal messages were being broadcast to the masses. Those who had more exposure to the messages were more likely to sit quietly while the government grew more powerful. Events that normally would have caused scandal and outrage went largely uncommented by the majority of the people until one day the people stopped noticing or caring at all.

"After the merger between the government and the media, the government mandated a switch to a visual media device that allowed subliminal messages to be broadcast into every home, sending a basic message of control, the population's resistance declined further until only a few were left who could still think for themselves.

"The education system – yes, there was an education system for the public, for everyone at one point in time – disintegrated into such a state that students learned more by *not* attending school. Government mandates and programs meant to help the education system hindered students that had both potential and motivation while failing the students the programs were meant to help.

"Disease and famine wiped out most of the African continent later on while natural disasters caused by government projects decimated much of the developed countries that might have proven difficult in the takeover by the global government. The world became such a polluted mess that it was impossible to survive. Madness and complacency became an everyday existence while those of us who tried to fight back were sent into hiding for fear of our lives… this is what the future will hold hundreds of years from now. So you see, you must listen to me. You can help to change it all."

"I refuse to hear your lies, demon," I tell it once more.

It stares at me, exasperated. I will not admit to it that its words have chilled me to the core. To believe the words would be madness, and I am certain of the lie.

"How did you come to the conclusion that one of the monks would help you?" I ask it.

"We didn't know," it says miserably. It slides down the wall of the tunnel and crouches with its hands covering its face for a long moment.

"I am unsure of your motives, demon. It is unclear how you came to choose this time and place, and the monks of our order."

"It was recorded. Written records. Solid evidence of someone being somewhere at a specific time," it says, its voice all but a moan.

"I do not understand."

"Most of the history we researched from the time period was an oral history later written down. The monks were different. You could read and write, and you documented important events in the monastery. The disappearance of 30 monks underneath the

Glastonbury Tor during a jaunt into the tunnels was noteworthy. We weren't sure of the exact time, so we've waited for your arrival."

"How many of your kind are here?" I ask and my voice is weak to my ears.

"Three of us have come to try to reason with you and your brothers. I fear we may have failed in our mission, however."

Two figures step from the darkness to stand over their companion. Their evil is almost palpable and the demon looks up to them expectantly.

"Well?" it asks hopefully.

They shake their heads in unison, then one speaks.

"I've been thinking…. What if…," it pauses and stares around as if searching for the right words. "What if we *change* some things?"

The demon uncovers its head and stares up at its fellow minion of hell. I am not comfortable with the light of understanding that has crept across the demons' features.

"How do you suggest we do that?" it asks its companion.

The second demon shrugs slightly. "We know what happens, and we know where it all went wrong. What if we fix it here so that when we return things will be different?"

The third demon begins to smile. "Brilliant. It would be a hell of a lot easier than trying to get through to these ones."

I do not like the way the third demon nods its head in my direction in reference to 'these ones'. The three demons turn toward me then, as if remembering that I am still there.

"What do we do with this one, then?" asks Norad.

"Same thing we'll do with the others," replies the second demon, "Only three monks come out. No one said *which* three or if their appearance was altered ... I think we can do this, since it doesn't seem to be working any other way...."

"Still, though," says Norad, "I don't feel right about it."

The third demon holds up a hand, interrupting Norad. "It's for the future."

The third demon nods and murmurs, "For the future."

***

To the person who finds this letter:

I want you to know, I tried. My intentions were good, and I tried…. And failed. My companions and I set out to heal a broken world, and I fear that we ultimately may be the cause of all that has gone wrong in the process.

Greed is part of the human condition, you see. No one is immune, not even me, for I was greedy for accolades and recognition. I was guilty of pride. Perhaps I would still be guilty of those things if I had not seen what my companions were really doing.

I have been guilty of all of the seven deadly sins. I can see that now. Indeed the road to hell is paved with good intentions, and I walked it so blindly. I thought myself more evolved than that lowly monk we left in the tunnels beneath the Tor. I believed that because we were stronger, we were right in our ambitions, but what hubris! How were any of us better than those we abandoned to starve to death or worse? We set out to end the problems of the world before they began, but now I see our error. My error.

It was my companions' plan the entire time not to fix the problems of the world, but to put themselves in power. When I attempted to stop them, I ended up here. Where and, more importantly, when 'here' is, I've no idea.

When I reflect upon the comments that society advanced quickly at the turn of the century – almost too quickly – I can't help but wonder if my companions had anything to do with it after they exiled me here.

We knew history, we knew what would happen… I can see now that Glastonbury Tor was merely an experiment, to see if our world changed as a result of our interference. We kept going back to 'rectify', my companions coming to the conclusion that the three monks who emerged from beneath the Tor were not actually the monks who had entered. When my resistance was clear, they convinced me to add a fourth member to the team – one who was more in line with their way of thinking. Once the fourth member joined our team, I was exiled. There really is no other word for it. When we were to return to our time and place, I woke to find myself beneath the ground still. I saw a staircase and followed it upward to discover that I was in a high stone tower, in the middle of a forest. I can hear ocean waves crashing in the distance, and that is all.

In the days that followed my initial exile, I attempted to contact my companions, to alert them of my location and time. As days passed, then weeks, I realized that my exile was intentional. I survived on what meager provisions were left with me, catching rain water in my clothing and eating the insects in the dirt cavern beneath this new tower.

I spent my days digging, my intent to break the surface and find the nearest human contact. That changed when humans found me as I looked out over the landscape from the top of the tower. Their shouts of fear and firing of guns and arrows at me was terrifying, and I retreated back into my underground haven.

The realization that I could not make contact with humans became clear over the course of years spent in exile beneath the tower. I tunneled more to pass the time than anything else. I made an exit for myself into a nearby clearing, where I was able to exit unseen and forage for berries and edible plants in the woods.

My appearance was something I had never thought about, hidden in the darkness as I was most of the time. My contact with fellow humans was limited and infrequent.

When a house was built near the tower, I dreaded that the family would discover my hiding place. My tunnels became deeper and more winding, in hopes that the humans would not find me.

During one of my tunnel excursions, I found myself watching two young people – a boy and a girl – explore the tunnels I had carved out of the dirt and rock. The girl was lovely, and my heart longed for human contact.

I heard her brother call her Rose, and thought how lovely and perfect a name it was. I found myself becoming slightly reckless on the days I knew she would wander alone through the tunnels. She almost caught sight of me several times.

One day, she did catch me. I was beyond caring at that point. Dare I say I had fallen in love with her after watching her for so long?

Her reaction was not typical. She didn't scream or run from me. In fact, I think she rather pitied me. She brought me clothes and food and books – BOOKS! I discovered I was in Maine, just before the Depression.

In spite of my appearance, and even my occasional rantings which must have sounded mad to dear Rose, she fell in love with me. I had never known love before I set out on my mission to set the world right. I had been a very young and very foolhardy man when my companions and I had built our time machine. It had always been my belief that I would have time for love later on, when the world was a better place.

While Rose and I were busy falling in love, the fourth member of our time-jumping group had an attack of conscience. He had been new to the team, so had not built up the resentment and hatred that my companions had felt toward me. After spending time as an impostor monk, I can also assume he found morals, to some extent. One day the fourth member of the group appeared to me in the tower. He was horrified by the changes I had undergone, and offered to travel back to the first days of my exile in order to rectify the situation. I told him I would not trade those days for anything, that I had finally found love, and for him to 'rescue' me would be to damn me to a life of loneliness and brooding.

We both understood that there was nothing we could do to stop our companions, but perhaps we might be able to salvage the future, that revolution was upon our time. He had traveled ahead to see how it all turned out, and ultimately good won.

The revolution was started by us he told me. I asked if I had a wife in the future he had seen. He nodded and said it was my lovely Rose.

We spent the day planning our return, and I waited to tell Rose my news.

When she found me I introduced her to my companion and explained what I must do. I told her that I would leave for one week, then return to her to see if she would like to come with me, as my wife.

Our week apart was hell, but there was so much to do in my own time that I rarely had time to feel lonely. I was working on a better future to bring my wife home to, after all.

When I returned, she was waiting for me. She had not packed any of her belongings, preferring to leave simply and with a clean slate. She said she had told her parents and brother that she loved them. Specifically to her brother she had said not to weep for her when she was gone, because she was not truly gone.

And so we have left, and I have left this note in hopes that her family will find comfort in it and that it will redeem me in the eyes of society. I am not and never have been a demon, only a fallen man.

I hope that if our paths cross again, it will be in a better future than the past I could not change.

-- Norad, 1910

SUNDOGS

By XIRCON

The sun was hot in the sky with several bright silver rings extending around it in a series of blinding colorless rainbows. Cain pulled the car off to the side of the road and closed his eyes against the glare off the dashboard. Why the hell was he here, he asked himself again. Had he gone stupid over the years? He had not lived as long as he had by doing stupid things, and yet here he was. Perhaps it was because he knew he had the equivalent of divine diplomatic immunity? Or was it the possibility of seeing something new after centuries of seeing only the same familiar things? He stared at the letter, read the words typed neatly across the corporate letterhead and knew them to be as false as the name and scrawled signature, yet something had drawn him to the old casino.

He re-read the enclosed newspaper clippings and a chill ran up his spine. The first article showed images of burned slot machines and the corpses of melted furniture. The story said the casino had been the 'target of a meteor shower'. Cain frowned at the strange wording and wondered if meteors could choose their impact zones.

The second and third articles had no pictures of the casino but they did show religious zealots holding aloft badly written signs with such catchphrases as 'REPENT!' and, Cain's personal favorite, 'GOD HATES fill-in-the-blank'. It amused him that the same congregations who preached about a just and loving God could flip the coin so easily between the Old and New Testaments. So quickly the love changed to vengeance based on jealousy with the turn of a sandwich board. He closed his eyes and hoped none of the demonstrators would be out when he arrived. He might just tell them what their God was really like. Just to be a dick.

Cain pulled the car back onto the empty road and continued his journey without thinking about his destination. When the building loomed into view he slowed down and stared at the sky for a few moments, unsure exactly of what he was looking for, but certain it was up there, waiting for him. Pulling his gaze from the sky and back to earth, to the shimmering asphalt, Cain felt a host of misgivings as he drove up to the casino. What the rumors and newspaper clippings had not accomplished, seeing the place first-hand did.

He slowed the car to a crawl then to a stop, scraping his nervous gaze across the stucco covering the outside of the building as he searched for signs of danger. He got out of the car and handed the valet his keys, dropping them into the kid's upturned palm. The missing fingers on the hand did not at first register.

"'Eye ow fer sundogs," the valet said

The words were misshapen and caught Cain's attention enough for him to register the missing digits on the kid's hand and he turned to face the valet. Their eyes locked and Cain's mouth went dry.

One eye stared out of the valet's face, the other was sealed beneath an avalanche of burn scars that spread from where the kid's left ear would have been to where the other half of his nose should have been. Cain tried not to cringe at the sight of the badly healed scars. He had been through enough over the years and seen more than his share of burn victims, but typically they had not stared back at him from the newspaper photos. He shook himself and gave a nod to the valet.

"Thanks, I will," Cain said. His voice came out weak and he cleared his throat. "Where can I find the manager?"

The valet gave a twitch that served as a nod and pointed the one finger that remained on his left hand in the direction Cain should go. Cain wondered if the kid was gunning for a better tip or if his right hand was in worse shape than his left. He did not bother to worry about the rental car or how the kid could drive. It was well insured, considering the reason he was there.

"Upsares, leff, leff, stray."

Cain nodded his thanks and handed the kid a twenty, waiting to see with which hand the kid would take the bill. Instead of reaching for the offered tip the kid twitched his head toward a metal box with a slot cut in the top. A yellow square on the side proclaimed TIPS in large black letters. Cain slid the twenty into the slot.

"Dankssir."

Cain tried not to think about how the valet had earned his scars or lost his digits as he made his way toward the entrance. He most definitely did not question how the kid would manage to park a car.

He climbed the stairs as the kid had directed, turned left then left again. He found himself staring down a long hallway leading to an almost stereotypical set of double doors. As if on cue one of the overhead fluorescents began to flicker.

"Perfect," Cain muttered and made his way to the double doors in quick strides.

Before he could raise his fist to knock there was a subtle click and the doors swung open. He stared across a vast expanse of Berber carpeting to the rosewood desk situated near a wall of windows that he guessed to be one-way mirrors.

"Please come in," said a quiet voice to his right.

Cain turned quickly to find an unassuming but large man in a suit. The man stood so close to him that Cain could smell the man's aftershave and something else. The scent was familiar and he realized with a shudder it was the smell of burned buildings and brimstone.

He gave a nod and followed the man to the desk. The man motioned to one of the two chairs in front of the desk, indicating he should have a seat.

"Mr. Lyle will be right with you," the large man said before retreating back into the anonymous shadows lurking in the corners of the room.

Security, Cain thought as he settled into a chair. He stared at the brass nameplate on the desk and smirked.

"Show yourself," he said to the room and filled the statement with as much command as he could muster.

The high-backed leather chair on the other side of the desk had been facing the window wall and there was a small creak when it sank as if with sudden weight. The chair tipped slightly, confirming occupation as it swiveled around to face him. Cain rolled his eyes at the trick meant to impress lesser men.

"You've been around too long, Cain," said the slender gentleman seated in the chair across from him, "I can remember a time when I would have terrified you with that entrance."

"People change," Cain said with a shrug, "But not you, you never change, do you? You have never been subtle."

The man raised an eyebrow, questioning.

Cain pointed to the nameplate. "B. Lyle. Really?"

The man let out a sound that might have been a laugh and shrugged. "It seems to work as effectively as Superman hiding behind a suit and ugly glasses so no one will recognize him," he said, eyes glittering.

"Enough, demon. What's the problem?"

"Very well," said Belial, "Enough of the charade."

The demon stood and its human form slid from its body like a shed snakeskin. Cain felt queasy as he stared at the discarded form that was crumpled on the chair.

The demon stretched and batlike wings unfurled from its back. Its neck crackled as it turned its head and stood up to its full height. Cain watched as the tiles on the drop ceiling whispered hollowly against Belial's hairless scalp.

"We have a bit of a situation, I'm afraid," the demon said, this time in its true voice. The sound of the words gave Cain the impression of listening to a room full of pit vipers lounging in a beehive. Belial went on, "I'm sure you've heard the rumors, and we have sent you the newspaper clippings."

Cain gave a neutral shrug. "If these things are for real, what is it you expect me to do?" he asked.

"As a start," the demon replied, "You might tell us what they *are*."

Belial motioned for Cain to follow him into a room filled with security monitors. One of the men manning a station turned at their entrance and Cain saw that this man was marked like the valet. Burn scars began at the back of the security man's head and ran around to his face in an angry pink slash as if he had turned to see what was burning him. The man seemed not to notice that his boss was a huge batlike creature, or possibly he was used to the sight of Belial in his true form. It was possible the demon only slipped on his skin suit when there was company.

"Mr. Dee, please punch up the footage for our friend."

The man's fingers flitted over a keyboard and one of the many monitors flickered. Cain turned his attention to the screen and waited. At first he saw nothing out of the ordinary. Patrons wandered in and out of the frame while some stopped at the slots.

About two minutes into the footage Cain turned to the demon. When he opened his mouth to speak Belial held up a long, clawed finger and pointed to the monitor. Cain noted with growing unease that the demon's gaze never strayed from the images on the screen. The look in those unearthly silver eyes was both intense and filled with terror.

With effort Cain pulled his attention away from the demon's face and back to the security feed. The hairs on the back of his neck prickled as the first patron paused with his hand raised and about to hit the buttons on the front of the slot machine at which he sat.

The man was in his mid-thirties Cain guessed, and his expression was one of confusion as he cocked his head to the side to listen. Over the next thirty seconds on the counter other slot players glanced up from their games as if they too heard something strange. At thirty-five seconds one of the patrons looked up at something off-camera and began to scream.

The hairs on the back of Cain's neck rose. He could feel the demon's stare intensifying next to him and found his own eyes riveted on the television.

"There," Belial whispered with a tone suggesting he had watched the feed several times.

As soon as the word left the demon's lips every patron in the frame was screaming in terror. Those who were able to run did so, leaving those who could not or who were not fast enough to face whatever was coming.

And then Cain heard his own voice shouting, "Sweet Christ! What the hell is it?!"

He was unaware he had been backing away from the security monitors until his back bumped into the door on the opposite side of the room. He lifted a cigarette to his lips and chased it with his mouth, unable to take it from his own shaking hands.

When he managed to take the cigarette he looked up to see Belial standing too close to him, the continued carnage playing on the security monitor behind him. The demon flicked its long nails and a flame appeared. Without a word it lit Cain's cigarette then met his gaze.

"Well?"

Cain took a long drag off his cigarette and looked anywhere but at the screaming faces. At last he shook his head.

"I have no idea what it is. I've never seen anything like it," he told Belial, "And you're sure it's not something from your department? Maybe some top secret project?"

The demon shook its head, its voice grave. "We have never created something like that to be unleashed upon this realm or even in our own domain. If we had, it certainly would not be attacking our establishments."

Belial pressed a button on what appeared to be an intercom. "Koth, please bring the others when you come in, will you?"

"Others?" Cain shifted uncomfortably.

"Eye witnesses."

The door opened and a small group of casino staff was ushered into the room by a man who suspiciously resembled Gregory Peck if he had managed to escape the confines of a black and white Noir film. Cain stared after the gray-skinned man for a moment before turning his attention back to the people before him.

Two men and two women looked at him with open curiosity, all eyes seeming to focus upon his forehead. Self-consciously he brushed the fringe of hair he kept in the front over the mark and focused upon the group. All of them had varying degrees of burn scars etched into their skin and faces, and all of their eyes held a haunted expression he had not seen in over a decade.

"Tell Mr. Cain what you saw," Belial said to them.

Cain looked up in surprise at the sudden change in the demon's voice only to see the demon was once more wearing his skin suit. He blinked at the speed of the transformation and the younger woman in the group cleared her throat to speak.

Her expression would have been fearful if half of her face had not been scarred to paralysis on one side. The tremble in her words communicated the emotion all too well, however.

"I saw 'em three months ago," she said and shot an unsure glance at Belial. The demon nodded for her to go on, and she continued, "I was working the floor, bringing drinks to folks…. The screaming," her voice trailed off into a whisper and she covered her mouth with a scarred hand as if to hold the memory at bay.

Her shoulders shook for a moment and Cain realized that she was sobbing. No tears fell from her scarred eyes, however, and the only indication of her pain was the silent, open-mouthed cries that refused to come out.

"The screams," she finally went on, "they made me look up and that's when I got this."

She motioned to her face and her voice hitched. Cain imagined if she had had any tear ducts left she would be noticeably crying.

"What exactly did you see?" he asked her, his voice gentle.

"Fire. It was everywhere and people were just," she motioned helplessly, "Just… they were ashes in the shapes of people!"

The older woman standing next to her nodded, her hands shaking as she comforted her companion. Cain observed her scarring was not as severe as the rest of the group's.

"What did you see?" he asked the older woman.

"It's like Cindy says, there was fire everywhere and then all these people that caught in it just turned to ashes. They screamed like hell as soon as the fire touched 'em, then they went all black as cinders, like they were burned statues. Then they just fell apart….. 'Least they went quick."

"What started the fire?" Cain asked and the two women shook their heads and shrugged.

"Wasn't started," said one of the men, "Was just there, running after people."

"Running?" Cain asked.

The man nodded.

"It's why we call them sundogs, sir," said the fourth member of the group.

His voice was quiet, as if he feared the repercussions of speaking too loudly about the disaster. His hair was shaped into a high and tight style and Cain guessed he was former military. Judging from the older scars across his face beneath the fresh burn scars, he had seen more than his share of death and horror.

"They looked a bit like a mastiff that was made of fire. They came through the ceiling like a rocket and started chasing people before they even hit the ground."

Cain took a slow breath, more to still his pounding heart than anything else. He felt for a moment as if he had been holding his breath.

"I guess we had better take a look at the main floor and see what we can find," he told Belial.

The demon gave a grim nod of agreement and motioned for Cain to follow him. When they were out of earshot of his staff, the demon turned to him and leaned in close.

"No lies. What the hell are these things?"

"I have no idea. I also have no idea why you called *me* in to take a look," Cain said.

"Because you've been around a long time and you've seen things we might not have. We don't spend all of our time top-side, you know."

They walked on in silence and Cain could smell the scent of a spent fire growing stronger. At last they came into an open area where slot machines stood derelict, some burned to cinders, others melted, and those that survived coated in black residue that grimed the screens.

Cain looked around in horrified awe, his gaze climbing the smoke-damaged walls and cauterized stairwells. Portions of a pedestrian walk above the floor were seared away to expose the beams and concrete within the metal frame. In spite of the supports being burned away, the catwalks remained suspended miraculously above the floor though the groan of strained metal and masonry could be heard clearly in the eerie silence around them.

The demon led him up a flight of stairs that remained intact and they edged their way carefully along the mezzanine. With each structural noise the bottom dropped a little more out of Cain's stomach and he feared he might be sick if they failed to leave soon. There was nothing here, no evidence of what had wreaked such havoc but video tape and survivors' tales.

"Why am I here?" Cain whispered.

His voice caught in his throat and the taste of burnt flesh and cinders mingled with the rising sickness on the back of his tongue. He leaned heavily against the wall and tried to gulp in air. The demon watched him for a moment and its eyes glittered silvery cold with curiosity.

"Damn you, why did you call me here?" Cain shouted into the demon's silence.

Belial's laugh was low, the deep notes rumbling through the stale and smoke-singed air. It raised its arms and the skin suit slid off its body in a fluid motion to pool at the demon's feet. Cain fell to his knees as the weakness overcame him. Every cell in his body told him to run, but his brain refused to send the required synaptic bursts through his nerves and muscles to enable escape.

"No earthly creature, be they animal, man, demon, nor angel could touch you," Belial hissed, "It was decreed and we had no choice but to abide by the Word This decision angered those of us who had been cast out for far lesser crimes, you see, and for millennia we have waited for our chance to bring you to the justice you so deserved."

The demon motioned to the space around them. Its smile slithered across its lips slick with a loathing that was palpable.

"We found that this place has something that no other place on this world has. Something very special. Something not of this world."

There was a sound in the distance that raised every hair on the back of Cain's neck. He strained to hear it over the demon's words, then realized in a few moments he would not have to strain. Whatever made the sound was coming closer.

"What is the point of all this?" Cain asked as he struggled to his feet. He leaned against the wall for support and backed away slowly.

"YOU are the point, Qayin, First Son of Adam. It is high time you paid for your crime, and at last we have discovered a way to allow that to happen."

The sound grew louder and the building shook with the vibration of its approach. Cain stumbled away from the demon and covered his ears against the increasing volume, but Belial dragged him to the edge of the mezzanine. With a small hop they sailed to the middle of the main floor and Belial released him.

The sound of his legs breaking as the demon struck him was drowned out in the howling that came from just beyond the ceiling of the casino floor. Cain's screams mingled with the howling, and as he stared up at the things crashing through the roof and into the blackened space blood trickled from his ears and nose.

The ringing in the silence was almost as bad as the howling of the things that blazed like a million fires. Cain could no longer hear his own screaming and knew without turning his gaze from the things approaching him that he was alone in the room with the sundogs. Footprints left in fire spread behind the fire dogs with every step they took, lighting the darkness with the yellow glow of torchlight.

The dogs were huge, like small horses with canine heads and paws. With each wag of their tails they sent burning embers into the shadows to set light to whatever they touched. Cain stared into the blood red orbs of the alpha and continued to scream. Where nothing else had been able to end him, he knew these things could. As he stared his eyes teared then bled, the light burning through his pupils and into his skull.

"What are you?" he whispered, his voice hoarse and stuttered with sobs of pain.

He was unable to look away despite the permanent damage being done to his vision. The creature cocked its head to the side as if in consideration, then sat back on its haunches. In a slow and fluid movement it stood as if it had been a man coming up from a crouch. The sound of bones dislocating and relocating was audible even over the sound of roaring fire and Cain cringed. When the transformation was complete a man engulfed in flames stood before Cain.

When it spoke its voice was filled with whispers and ashes, gravelly and harsh with fire. Flames burst forth from its lips with every plosive, the sparks raining down upon Cain like Napalm.

"We are vengeance and retribution," it said, "We are the cleansing fire in the wake of the flood. We are the scorched earth settled to salt."

Two other sundogs moved to join their alpha, flanking the burning man. They stared down at Cain and growled low in their throats.

"You have walked the earth for far too long without knowing fear," the thing continued, "We are here to show you all the terror you deserve."

Cain stared, his vision blackening at the edges as the thing took another step closer. With a growing sense of dread, he realized his eyes had dried to the point he could no longer close them. His skin was becoming tight where it was exposed to the flames, fluid rushing in to protect the meat beneath. He opened his mouth to speak, but no words could escape his parched throat. If he could have spoken, he would have told them he was afraid. For the first time in millennia he was terrified.

The burning man moved closer and Cain let out a silent cry of agony. He willed his body to move, to escape, but he was paralyzed by fear. All he could do was stare into the light of the sundogs.

The scent of burning hair reached his nose and he realized it was his own as his eyelashes curled and shrank until only wisps were left to fall away from his face. Not like this, he thought, not with fire. Anything but fire!

The skin of his face cracked, the burn blisters weeping like tears down his cheeks. The fear paralysis finally broke and Cain dragged himself backward, away from the burning things and their heat. The burning man watched him go and Cain dared to believe he might escape this hell.

He moved faster, the skin on his hands cracking and falling away in smears across the floor. He wished he had something to drink, but that could come later when he was away from these things. It never occurred to him to wonder why they were not following him or even trying to prevent him from escaping, he assumed the point had been to scare him and injure him, not kill him. Nothing ever killed him.

The back of his head hit the wall and Cain let out a breath that could have been a groan if he had had a voice left. He turned his head to see if there was a way out and felt the skin on the front of his neck break open. There was no way out but to go through the sundogs.

The burning alpha walked toward him in slow, deliberate strides that left footprints of fire in their wake. It closed the distance between them and Cain sobbed as it leaned in close. It took hold of his face and Cain sucked in a breath filled with flames. As the fire reached out to stroke his face he could see the features of the man more clearly. If he had had eyelids left they would have gone wide with recognition.

"At last you recognize me, my brother," said Abel.

THE LAZARUS STONE (CONSPIRACY EDIT)

By XIRCON

PROLOGUE: THE BEGINNING OF THE END

At first the explosions on the horizon could have been mistaken for a particularly red sunrise. Standing on the beach and drinking what he considered to be his last coffee, he savored the bitter black heat as it poured over his tongue to warm his belly. The cool feel of sand between his bare toes, the feel of the last non-toxic breeze – all of these things he felt and committed to memory. He even relished the sharp pain in his eyes as he stared at the glow on the horizon and the wet feel of the only tears he would shed coursing down his cheeks with each watery blink. Finally he broke free of the nuclear trance and with a dread he had never felt before he ran to his truck. Within minutes he was home and locked in his bomb shelter.

The electricity didn't last long. By the light of a camping lantern and with shaking hands he re-read the last letter he would ever receive. When he finished reading he stared at the picture enclosed.

Carefully he traced the woman's face in the photo then set it and the letter aside. He pulled on his fatigues, tearing his name patch and military branch label off the front of the uniform and flushing them down the chemical toilet. Letting out a ragged breath, he turned out the lantern and waited for the end of the world to find him.

CHAPTER 1

The world had not ended. He stared at the crackling radio, but no stations were on air. The last live voice he had heard before the final nuclear strike was that of the president urging everyone to remain calm and seek shelter. He wasn't sure how he had known when the last bomb had hit, but he seemed to feel it. The president's voice faded into horrified shock, followed by dead air.

At least a month had passed since the last broadcast. He tracked time with an old wind-up watch and a calendar covered by stacked marker-made X's. He marked off the last day of the month and flipped to the next. His eyes stared through the pastoral scene that indicated the arrival of June.

A quick calculation of his rations assured him he would have enough food to last well into the next June. The shelves in his shelter held plenty of vitamin supplements and he had fitted his new home with full spectrum fluorescent lights. An exercise bike stood in one corner, cables connected from the stationary bike's wheel to a small generator.

Stacks of books covered one wall from floor to ceiling. Topics ranged from technical, how-to, languages, and finally fiction novels.

Through a small door was a tiny bathroom fitted with a chemical toilet and potable water tank. A filtration system on the tank assured recycled water for bathing. The ventilation was a simple Kearny Air Pump system. His main living area was double-walled to create a space for airflow and as a secondary sediment-catcher. The intake vent was mounted in a dirt mound on the surface and reinforced beneath the dirt with sandbags and cinder blocks. The pull-chord and flap setup provided enough airflow for the small space to stay relatively bearable during the day.

His cot was set up close to both the bunker's entrance and his gun cabinet. The cabinet was metal and contained a small collection of concealable weapons with boxes of 9mm rounds. Beneath his pillow was a sheathed hunting knife, and throughout the bunker there were items that could easily become weapons if needed. The rest of his weapons – knives mostly – were secured to his body, under his clothes.

Beneath his cot was an array of medical supplies in meticulously labeled office supply boxes. One box contained various sizes of bandages and ace wraps, splints, and sterile gauze. Another contained antibiotics, cough syrup, cold medications, and antibiotics. A third box contained ointments, alcohol, iodine, and hydrogen peroxide. Also in the box were bags of sterilized syringes and glass bottles filled with morphine. Several pill bottles contained Vicodin and many more held aspirin.

Each day he got up and pumped the air through the bunker, then did countless repetitions of jumping jacks, pushups, pull-ups, and sit-ups before pedaling the exercise bike to generate the day's electricity. His meals in the first weeks were military rations that had their own chemical heating elements included in the plastic packages. Most of his time he spent pacing within the small space or reading his books. At the end of each day he worked the pull chord of the ventilation system then crossed off another square on his calendar before turning off the lights.

Each night he stared up into the darkness and wondered what he would find when he ventured back to the world above him.

CHAPTER 2

The letter and the picture were worn ragged when he made the decision to exit his shelter. He had allowed two months to pass to ensure that fallout and radiation were at 'acceptable' levels. He crossed off the last day of the second month and sighed. What good was surviving if he was the only one left alive?

He carefully unfolded the letter and read the neatly written words one more time. With equal care he re-folded the page into the envelope and stared at the picture. The woman in the picture wasn't smiling, yet everything about her seemed to smile. She was staring off to the side of the photograph, a notebook opened across her lap and a pen grasped delicately in her hand.

She used to sit like that for hours, the pen tapping her lips as she considered what would be recorded in the notebook. He had snapped the picture on a trip they taken to the mountains. She said the mountains recharged her batteries and the ocean helped her forget. He never asked what she needed to forget and she never told him.

He wondered suddenly if she was still alive. The thought rushed in, unbidden and filled him with dread. Each day he read the letter and looked at the picture, but he had not allowed the thought to surface. He clung to the hope that the country had been protected somehow; that when he emerged from his shelter he would find rebuilding and cleanup efforts instead of a wasteland that held no signs of life or bodies. The thought that *she* might be among the dead disturbed him. There was so much left unsaid between them, so many questions left unanswered.

"Fuck it."

He started at the sound of his own voice. It sounded foreign to his ears and he realized he had not spoken in months.

That night he gathered supplies into a backpack. It would be a short trip – just an hour – to see if there was anything left. If there were survivors, he wanted to be sure he had protection in case they had gone feral in the aftermath.

The next day he opened the lead-lined steel door into the skeleton of what had once been his basement. He shifted the gasmask on his face, re-checked the straps, then climbed into the cracked foundation. He held a Geiger counter out and monitored the clicks. The levels seemed to be 'acceptable'. He looked around him and let out a breath. The sky was overcast with a reddish hue in the distance just over the basement wall horizon. The basement stairs led up to nothing and were charred. He would not have trusted the stairs or a floor to hold his weight, anyway.

He pulled himself up and over the remnants of the foundation and stared. The small town was all but gone. A few remnants of the older stone houses still stood, but all newer stick built houses were gone. He now had an unobstructed view of the ocean. He could just make out pieces and sections of sidewalk beneath dust and debris as he walked what would have been three or four blocks to the beach. His combat boots crunched over broken seashells and the bones of various creatures great and small before finally reaching the sand-glass of the beach.

As he neared the ocean a sense of foreboding filled him. He stopped ten feet from the water, unsure of why he felt so uneasy. He looked behind him, but all he could see were his footprints punched into the crust of the beach.

He turned his glance back to the waves and noticed the ocean was black. The surf moved like crude oil over the melted sand before sliding backward and away. There was something intelligent in the motion and he stepped back until he had added three or four more feet to the distance between himself and the surf. Try as he might, he found no comfort in the ocean any longer, and he didn't trust the tide.

With a shiver he turned and walked in-land to where the center of town had been. There was nothing left but the Courthouse and the ruins of two stone churches.

He explored the buildings and only found the rotted remains of the community huddled in the basements. No survivors. No animals. There was nothing left for him here.

He glanced at the sky then at his watch in disbelief. Instead of his planned hour, he had spent the better part of a day exploring. His steps betrayed an unconscious sense of urgency as he made his way back toward his shelter. He scanned the landscape, searching for his house.

In the distance he could hear the dull roar of the ocean, but it sounded strange, dangerous, as if it was not a body of water but a predator growling in the approaching evening. He checked his watch again and noted that the tide would be coming in. Instinct told him that he needed to be safely sealed in his bunker when the tide came in, even though he was well away from the shoreline.

His already hurried steps turned into a run. He reached the edge of the basement just as a rolling blackness slid over what remained of the sand dunes. He climbed into the foundation and slammed the door of his shelter just as the waves crashed above him. He threw the locks home and overhead the ocean howled with rage.

Sleep was impossible that night and the bunker was uncomfortably warm. He had been afraid to work the ventilation system, unwilling to give those black waves a chance to slither into his shelter. He could feel the ocean waiting in the darkness above.

CHAPTER 3

He didn't venture outside again for days. After a night of insomnia he made a list of necessities for a trip to Washington, D.C. then spent the next three days packing.

When he left he sealed his shelter behind him and began the long walk to the west. He knew that he would most likely need to head to Virginia, into the networks of caves there if he hoped to find anyone alive. He would stop in D.C. first, though, and see if there was anything or anyone left, then check the shelter in Pennsylvania before moving back down and into Virginia.

He walked for two days before reaching the Ben Franklin Bridge. Just beyond the bridge he could see Philadelphia. The city was surprisingly intact and eerily quiet.

He discovered that what remained of the city's last inhabitants lay sprawled and dead in the subway tunnels and in traffic jams throughout the city.

He made his way toward 13th and Chestnut Streets where he knew a military surplus store to be. He looked around him and saw that most of the glass was broken out of the storefronts as well as from the Liberty Place towers and other office buildings. Cars littered the streets, some with drivers rotting behind the wheel. He buried his anger deep, wondering who was responsible for the first punch that had started and completed World War 3 in a matter of hours.

Glass crunched under his boots as he stepped through the display front of the surplus store. He traded his worn combat boots for a new pair and picked out a sweater and a coat for the oncoming colder weather.

Canned meat and fruit were gotten in a burned out grocery store along with sardines and tuna. These new supplies would be last resorts once he ran out of his military rations.

He spent that night on the roof of an old apartment building overlooking the heart of Center City. He scanned the night below for any signs of life. There was nothing. The radio he had taken from the surplus store let out the occasional crackle over dead air.

The next morning he set off down Pine Street, then cut over toward South Street. At 3rd and South he paused to stare up at the worn mural of Larry Fine.

He took the letter out of his breast pocket and checked the return address. He knew her apartment was across the street, but he checked it again to be sure. He pushed the security gate out of the way and entered the apartment building. He paused on the landing outside of her place, listening for any sounds. His hand felt like lead as he lifted it to knock. No answer. The door to her apartment was locked.

He took out a lock pick set and used them on the door. The air inside her apartment was cool and stale. The skylights allowed some light in, but were so covered in dust that it made the apartment seem darker than usual. He took out a flashlight and shone it down the narrow hallway. Pictures still hung on the walls and all of her decorations were still in place as if she had stepped out to get groceries.

The bedroom told a different story, however. Clothes were scattered over the floor and bed. He could still smell her perfume in the room. It was a dark amber scent with a hint of musk. He glanced at her dresser and noticed the framed photographs weren't there. The cat carrier she kept in the closet was also gone, along with the cat and its owner. She had packed quick and light, and taken only the necessities.

He let his breath out slowly, not realizing he had been holding it the entire time. He checked the rest of the apartment and the basement, but found no sign of her. She wasn't there and he was glad, even relieved. It meant she might still be alive and out there somewhere.

He stepped back out onto South Street and followed it to the pedestrian bridge that spanned over I-95. He climbed down onto the highway and went south, making his way toward the capitol.

He followed the highway until he reached Wilmington, where he encountered similar carnage that he had found in Philadelphia.

He spent the night on the rooftop of an office building. No signs of survivors greeted him from the darkness below. Even the scent of rot and burning buildings no longer phased him.

The gas mask had been shoved into his backpack just after leaving Philadelphia. The Geiger counter went off if he strayed from the asphalt of the highway, so he stayed on the asphalt. He had been relieved to breathe without the mask, but he kept it with him, just in case. The road to D.C. was a long one, and he wasn't sure exactly what he would encounter, nor was he sure if there had been other attacks.

His next break before crossing the Maryland border was in Newark, Delaware. Near Aberdeen he set up camp and took stock of his food and water supplies. He was relieved to find an underground store of food and water at the military base. Judging by the sprawl of bodies, the attacks had come as a surprise for everyone. The casualties were not as numerous on the base however, leading him to conclude that the majority of the personnel had been mobilized to defend the capitol.

He spent the night in Aberdeen, then started out a little before sunrise, once more following I-95 south. He wondered if all the roads were jammed by bodies at the wheels of dead cars, or if it was just the main highways.

In Baltimore he found himself drawn to the aquarium. He broke through the doors and walked quietly through the cool darkness. He took out his flashlight and shone it into the tanks, then frowned. The fish were all gone. He cocked his head to the side for a moment, his lips pressed in a confused line. He aimed the light upwards, searching the murky water and froze. The bodies shimmered in the beam of light as if they were moving and it took him a moment to realize his hand was shaking. These were the first actual bodies of animals he had seen. In New Jersey there had been bones left by the tide, but the aquarium fish were unmolested by a predatory ocean.

He moved upward toward where the tanks opened at the top and staggered back at the scent of bleach permeating the air. He felt sick suddenly. It was as if they dead fish in the aquarium had made his situation real to him. He rushed outside, back into the open, and sucked in huge gulps of air, fighting back the urge to vomit.

The sidewalk rose up to meet him and he sat hard. He ran a shaking hand over his face, tracing scars he had gotten as a child and those he had received as an adult. Mingled with the scars were the fine lines of age.

"Get a grip," he told himself.

His voice was little more than a whispered growl, but it felt good to hear the words out loud and it felt good to say them. He sighed and leaned back until he was flat on his back and staring up at the sky.

Clouds still hung angry and gray above him. He wondered if he would ever see the sun again, then decided it wasn't important.

He climbed to his feet, hoisted his backpack, and left Inner Harbor as fast as he could. He spent the night overlooking

Baltimore's dark skyline, and at sunrise he was back on I-95 and walking toward Washington.

CHAPTER 4

D.C. was worse than he had expected. He still had a distance to go before he reached Washington, D.C. proper, but judging from the lack of buildings and the piles of cars left in blackened heaps, he didn't need to see his nation's capitol to know there was no one left alive. It was obvious there had been more than one attack, and Washington had been a target. He diverted off his original course to pick up the Beltway to Route 1. The charred landscape began a few hundred yards along Route 1 off the Beltway.

He stared at the crater where a metropolis had been. The possibility that he would encounter this very scene had stayed at the front of his mind during his entire journey, but seeing it was another thing entirely. His knees buckled and he dropped to the asphalt. Try as he might, he couldn't seem to get enough air.

He fell to all fours, willing his chest to unlock, for his pulse to slow. It was useless. His vision darkened and he tried to laugh at the irony that he might be having a heart attack after having survived the apocalypse. He welcomed the blackness when it overtook him.

***

He regained consciousness slowly. He judged from the fading light that he had been out for approximately two hours. His watch read six o'clock when he focused on it, confirming his theory, and he let out a slow breath before winding it. What he had feared to be a heart attack he realized was an emotional overload, possibly a panic attack. Still, the very real possibility of a medical emergency and no one to help him loomed very real in the back of his mind. More than ever he wanted to get to Pennsylvania. He only hoped when he got there he would find someone alive.

He pulled off his combat boots and socks and winced at the feel of blisters. He tugged his bag open and pulled out a first aid kit. He had brought plenty of antibiotic ointment and bandages, along with travel size bottles of peroxide and alcohol. He cleaned off the popped blisters and applied ointment, then covered the spots with bandages.

He would camp here, he decided. Each day he had pressed on without considering the physical and mental exertion. It had finally caught up to him and he realized he needed to rest, then come up with a new plan.

He set up his tent and leaned on his backpack once inside. The asphalt was hard beneath the nylon floor of the tent, but it was reassuring somehow. He rested his bare feet against the cool hardness and opened a well-worn copy of a book he had been forced to read in high school. The cover had fallen away years ago, along with the title page. He lifted the book to his face and pressed his nose into the pages. The scent was vaguely musty, like an old library, but comforting in a way he could not explain. He wished now for a library that he could escape into, if only for an hour. He reminded himself again that should he come across a library, he should not consider taking books, as they would most likely be saturated in radiation and fallout.

No more books but the ones he had brought. The thought was a sobering one. In the world before the nightmare he now lived, he had not been considered a reader, even to himself. With the realization that the world could erupt in war, he had gone to the local library and bought books on the library funding/donation racks. He carried a few of those titles with him now along with some he had checked out the week before the end of the world. The irony that the majority of the titles were stories about nuclear war and the apocalypse did not escape him.

That night he read by the glow of a chemlight. The stillness outside the tent was eerie. No sound of insects, animals, or people, just a moaning wind that seemed to make the night all the quieter when it died down.

His dreams were nightmares and he woke drenched in sweat with a scream still bitten behind his lips throughout the night. At 5am he took out the roadmap and reviewed his notes as well as the placement of the circles he had drawn to indicate stopping points. There were stars scrawled over Aberdeen, Washington, and a small mountainous region not far from Frederick, MD. He traced his finger over the Beltway to Rte 270, then upward along the map to Rte 15. He decided that regardless of what he found when he reached the last star on his map, he would set up camp in the caves and hope to find enough food to last the rest of his life.

The world was just beginning to brighten when he finished packing the tent and cleaned up the remnants of his breakfast. When he set out there was no trace of him left behind.

He reached Frederick around sunset, or at least around what passed for sunset. The buildings at the outskirts of the city were broken and crumbling, giving evidence that the bomb that had hit Washington had most likely been detonated further inland and lower to the ground, as Baltimore and Aberdeen had been largely unscathed.

An abandoned office building served as his rest stop. He reapplied ointment to the blisters on his feet and changed the bandages, then settled in for the night.

Once more the nightmares woke him. He sat up, sure that he had heard voices. He shoved the chemlight under his sleeping bag to hide the light without knowing why. He ran to the edge of the roof and looked down, straining to hear a sound. There was nothing. He let out a rush of breath and walked back to his tent and sleeping bag. He was unsure if he was disappointed or relieved.

The next morning he slept in until a quarter to nine. He stopped halfway through rushing to break down his camp and laughed at himself. Why was he hurrying as if he would be late? It was not as if anyone knew he was alive, nor would they expect him at a certain time. Old habits, he mused as he put away the last of the items.

By 9am he was back on the road, following 270 toward 15. He reached Raven Rock Mountain at 7pm and set up camp in the middle of a playground. A perimeter fence was visible, razorwire swirling around the top like killer curls. The next day he would follow the fence to the entrance, then hope to God someone was there.

That night he read a few more pages of his book by chemlight. Though the nights had finally started to cool, he thought it best not to light a fire. The trees were dry from the lack of rain and he didn't think it was prudent to start a fire that could end up engulfing the entire east coast.

Upon inspection of his blisters, he was glad they appeared to be healing. He applied ointment, but left the bandages off for the night so the wounds could breathe.

He woke from a dead sleep and stared into the darkness. Panic seized him and he grabbed at the ground, fingers searching for the chemlight. He shoved it under his sleeping bag and held his breath. There was a loud snap as of an animal stepping on a twig and he had his gun out and aimed before he had time to think about the action. He unsnapped the leather clasp holding his hunting knife in its sheath and flinched at the noise of the snap. Carefully he slid the knife out and set it on the ground next to him.

There was another crackle from the other side of the tent. He pulled out a second handgun and turned off the safety, holding both weapons aimed in the directions of the sounds from outside. He suspected what he heard was an animal, and was probably hungry or dying, but there was no sense taking stupid risks. If it was a deer, he was fine, but a bear, coyote, or even a mountain lion could pose a serious potential threat. He relaxed only slightly when he heard the sounds moving further from the tent on one side, but continued to aim the gun in his right hand toward the sound that had come from the opposite side. He could hear something breathing, and it was close.

It circled the tent to the opening flap and he stayed perfectly still. He continued to breathe as if still asleep while aiming the gun at the opening.

The zipper began to move slowly, opening the flap. He could hear its progress in the darkness and he felt the ground for his flashlight. He followed the zipper's progress with his eyes while aiming both gun and flashlight at the widening opening.

When he heard the flap being pulled back he clicked on the flashlight and yelled "Don't move!"

He fought back a grin as the man in night vision goggles screamed with surprise and pain. He followed the intruder into the open, tracking the other man's movements with both gun and light. Footsteps crashed toward them in the underbrush and he steeled himself.

"Don't move or your friend dies!" he yelled at the group of men running toward him.

They stopped just outside the beam of the flashlight, guns trained on him. He wondered briefly if they were loaded. One of the men stepped out from the group, his hands held up to show they were empty.

"Just relax," the man said smoothly, his voice even, "You are a soldier, yes?"

The accent in the words was subtle, but it was there. What was it? Ukrainian? British? French? He gave a quick nod in answer, never taking his eyes off of his prisoner or the group of men surrounding him.

"Who are you?" he asked.

His own voice sounded foreign to his ears. It had been months since he had spoken to anyone.

"We are survivors, like you," the man told him.

He considered the words. If they had wanted him dead they could have just opened fire on the tent while he slept, no questions asked.

There was a sharp crack of a branch behind him and he spun, gun raised, but too late. All he had done was give the shooter a better shot at his heart.

CHAPTER 5

"How do you think he survived?"

"How the hell should I know? Probably the same way we did."

His head hurt and the lights shining through his eyelids was far too bright. He remained still, his breath even and slow. He moved his fingers slightly to search out his knife and gun, but they were gone.

He felt the two men move closer to him, leaning over him. He fought the urge to reach up and crush their throats in his bare hands.

"No burns or lesions."

"Yeah… lucky him."

"He should be waking up soon."

"Mmmm. Any ID on him?"

"No, but he's military."

The other man let out a heavy sigh. "Poor bastard…. Alert me when he comes around. I want to talk to him."

"No need. He's awake." His voice came out rusty and gruff.

He could feel both men pause at his words. He suspected there may even have been a nervous glance exchanged. He turned so that his eyes were no longer facing the lights.

"What the hell did you hit me with? My head's killing me."

"Sorry about that. You apparently posed quite a threat."

"So kill me," he said with a frown, "Why keep me alive?"

"We needed answers."

He let out a grunt that was half laugh and half incredulous. *They* needed answers?

The two men backed up a step as he rose and he smirked. His bare feet made no sound as he walked to the table in the middle of the room where his bag was opened and emptied over the surface.

"Got any food and water?" he growled.

"Of course."

He shielded his eyes from the overhead fluorescents and stared at the two men. They seemed surprised by his request. He rifled through the contents on the table until he found his first aid kit. He popped the lid on a container of aspirin and dry-swallowed two. He looked around for his boots and pulled them on, quick-tying the laces around the ankle of the boot.

The men watched him quietly, their eyes burning a hole into his back. Without turning to face them he said, "You've got questions, so do I. Let's trade answers over a meal."

"That's a great idea, mister…. I'm sorry. We don't know your name."

"Name's not important."

"You were clearly in the military…."

He gave a short nod as they walked through a sterile corridor. There was no carpeting, and their footfalls echoed as dull and gray as their surroundings. It looked like a Hollywood set for a high-end military bunker, he mused.

"So are we," the first man said. He was shorter than his companion, and he had already earned the secret nickname 'Highstrung'. "Which branch were you in?"

"The best one," he said with a wry smile, "but it doesn't seem to matter anymore now, does it?"

They entered a mess hall and moved through the subdued line of men. Some wore uniforms and more than a few wore suits. All looked as if they had not slept in weeks.

A tall man with broad shoulders wearing a dark blue suit approached them. He gave a nod in way of greeting. His face said he had bad news to tell.

"Gentlemen."

Highstrung paled at the man's grave expression. "Is he—?"

Dark Blue Suit nodded slowly.

"When?" the other man of the pair spoke up. He had been dubbed 'The Thinker' because he seldom spoke.

"About fifteen minutes ago. He'd been too exposed. The medics were surprised he lasted this long."

"Jesus wept…. Now what are we going to do?" Highstrung asked

"There's the other option," Suit said quietly.

Thinker turned toward him and indicated that he should remain in the line of men moving through the mess hall. "If you'll excuse us. We have some things to talk about. Why don't you get a nice hot meal and we'll join you in a few minutes?"

The suit motioned the two men away and only a few words were discernable. He could feel their eyes on him as he continued through the food line and knew part of the conversation was about him. When he had filled his tray he searched out an empty table and sat down. While Suit talked to Highstrung and Thinker he scanned the room.

Every face wore a haunted expression; every man seemed to go through the motions of eating. If anyone spoke, it was in hushed tones. It was the quietest mess hall he had ever seen. He frowned, the fine lines of his face deepening. There was something missing, something important. He searched the room and attempted to identify the missing element. Whatever was missing, it bothered him on a subconscious level. He shoveled a forkful of re-hydrated mashed potatoes into his mouth and scowled. The thought danced on the edge of his grasp and he jabbed at the vegetables in his plate.

The three men joined him without invitation, interrupting his thoughts. Their faces were grim and pale. He stared into their lackluster eyes and sighed. Whatever the news was, it was bad.

Suddenly he realized what was missing and he asked, "Where are the women?"

The men stared at him and their collective expression was one he did not like. It told him that he had confirmed their fear.

"You saw none on your travels here?" Thinker asked.

He realized now that Thinker had been the man with the hint of a foreign accent the night he had been taken to the bunker. He shook his head and shoveled another spoonful of mashed potatoes into his mouth. His arched eyebrow served to say for him 'If there had been any survivors, wouldn't I have brought them here with me?'

"There are no women here," Suit told him.

He kept his face and voice neutral. "Why not? Is there a separate living space for women?"

"No, no other space but here. The women… disappeared," Highstrung said before Suit glared him into silence.

"Disappeared? Like poof! Or one night they all up and went to get their hair done and never came back?"

The men's expressions grayed. He was suddenly having difficulty swallowing around the lump rising in his throat. Whatever had happened, he was not sure he wanted to hear it.

"All women and pets," Highstrung began, then said defiantly to Suit's stare, "He might as well know!" The small man cleared his throat and averted Suit's gaze before continuing. "Just before the... event," he continued, "we received reports of women, children, and larger animals disappearing. Country-wide. Witnesses said one minute they were there and having conversations and then nothing. Pets went the same way."

He let his utensils drop into his tray, his appetite gone. He understood the haunted expressions of the men now.

"No notes or anything?"

"Nothing. In all cases the disappearance was sudden and unplanned. Food left burning on stoves, showers and bathtubs left running. All of them were just... gone."

"Roanoke," he whispered.

The men nodded solemnly and stared into their untouched trays of food. He watched them silently for a moment, pushing the rest of his mashed potatoes and stuffing around.

"OK... so what the hell happened to the rest of the country?" he asked.

The men looked at each other, embarrassed. Suit finally cleared his throat.

"Where did you come from? What was the landscape like on your way here?"

"New Jersey. Specifically, near the shore. I came through some major cities. No survivors. Gridlock as far as roadways. I

checked the subways, but there were only bodies. So I ask again.…..
what the hell happened?"

"There was a… mistake," Suit said lamely.

"No shit."

Suit glared at him for a moment then continued, "We were in
the process of developing a counterstrike system to protect the
country in case of nuclear assault."

"Ahh… well, it all makes sense now."

Suit sighed. "Look, obviously shit hit the fan, but we could
never have anticipated this level of destruction."

"Really? Did you never watch a movie?" he said and flicked at
his fork in exasperation. "So what now? We just sit here and wait for
the damned food to run out?"

Suit stared at him as if he had said something that had never
occurred to him. He straightened his jacket and leaned closer.

"There was a last resort contingency," Suit went on, "a plan
F, if you will. Our researchers had developed an anti-weapon before
it all went down. During the commotion the anti-weapon was
launched. Our last communication with it showed it to have landed
somewhere near the shore in New Jersey."

"You do realize that New Jersey has a lot of shoreline to
cover, right?"

"Luckily, we have a guide."

CHAPTER 6

"What I'm about to tell you is highly classified."

He rolled his eyes at the suit and let out a brief laugh.

"What the hell's so funny?"

"Seriously? Even at the end of the world there's 'classified' information? Just get on with it. There's no one left out there to tell, I assure you."

Suit glared at Thinker and Highstrung as if to ask why they had brought him to Suit's attention at all. Suit placed his hands firmly on the tabletop and let out a slow breath.

"There is a contingency plan. The anti-weapon was supposed to have been launched into the ocean, which would have helped to 'heal' the damage of a nuclear assault. Obviously, we missed the mark by a bit."

"How much."

"We're not quite sure. Perhaps only a mile, perhaps more. All we know is that it's not in the ocean where it needs to be."

"So the plan is to venture out now that you know it's safe, find this 'anti-weapon' and get it to the ocean?" he asked skeptically.

Suit nodded.

"Do you know specifically around where this thing fell?"

"We think around Tom's River."

He whistled. "The Pine Barrens? Good luck."

"You won't help us?" Highstrung asked.

"I didn't say that. Just letting you know that the Barrens have a reputation."

The men looked at him blankly.

"The Jersey Devil?" he asked incredulously, "Or did you think there was just a Satanic hockey team?"

The men blinked, not getting his joke.

"Nevermind," he said, "Count me in for the mission. Not like I've got anything better to do, right?"

"There is one more thing," Suit added.

"Naturally."

The plan was outlined in great detail and preparations were made to leave first thing in the morning. A group of men were assembled who would accompany him on the trip. They looked scared by the idea of leaving the safety of their shelter. He was not surprised by their reactions at all. He was surprised when a stretcher with a corpse wrapped in canvas was brought out to join the small party.

"What the hell is this?" he asked.

"NO ONE is to uncover this body until you reach your destination. Is that understood?"

"You expect us to carry a body around with us?"

"Yes."

"How dead is it?" he asked and wondered if it was even a valid question. Dead was dead, after all.

Suit stared at him coldly, and without a trace of humor said, "He died yesterday."

"What do we do with it once we get to our destination?" he asked while shoving a gas mask into his pack.

"We bury him."

***

Three days later and the body they carried with them was starting to smell. The sickly-sweet, cloying stench of rotting meat wafted through the sun-baked air and the weaker-stomached members of their group covered their faces with scarves doused in perfume.

Their accusing eyes glared in the direction of the body and its carriers, but no words were uttered in opposition of their companions' motives. They had all agreed to do this.

They were a small group in comparison to the others that had preceded their current steps. Most of them had been high-ranking officers and officials of their respective governments at one time, now they looked like a band of nomads as they wandered through the fallout of the desert they had created, their rusted medals clinking and glinting from their sandblasted uniform breasts. The Holy Trinity of Suit, Highstrung, and Thinker had abandoned the cause early on, when they saw what was left of Washington, D.C. Some people had no stomach for the destruction they caused when they were confronted with it in person instead of on a monitor.

He adjusted his pack and scanned the horizon, squinting through the rising wind. He pulled the gas mask out of his pack and pulled it on. The men looked at him curiously until the warning went up.

"Storm," one of the men muttered hoarsely, a shaking finger raised to the horizon.

The others followed his pointing finger and those that had not covered their faces because of the reeking body now covered their faces against the incoming cloud of dust that moved toward them like a filthy tidal wave. The more fortunate among the men tugged goggles or gas masks down over their eyes and stared in morbid fascination at the oncoming sandstorm. The rest of the group quickly scanned the area for shelter, immediately running for the cluster of burnt-out buildings that had once served as a city.

The group huddled together over a small fire inside the basement remainder of an old brownstone. Scattered toys and burnt remnants of boxes and clothing littered the floor, the melted plastic eyes of the toys staring with silent blame at their new companions.

He stared into the flickering darkness with a small shiver of unease, his eyes meeting the half-melted stare of a charred teddy bear before quickly looking away. He shook the sand out of his gas mask and settled to the floor. Judging from the falling sand and masonry, he thought it would be a good idea to keep his goggles and the gas mask close at hand, just in case.

"This place gives me the creeps," he mumbled grudgingly.

His companions looked around them as if seeing where they were for the first time. They sat on fallen pieces of stone and concrete, cinderblocks, bricks and mortar among relics of a past they no longer remembered or had chosen to forget. Dust coated the basement as if nature had tried to bury the dead, and sand had started to seep into the cracks and corners, slowly covering the civilization that had once thrived on the spot. Their fire cast an eerie glow that sent ghosts and shadows dancing into the darker recesses of fallen masonry with a hiss of anger at the intruders.

"It feels like a tomb," one of the men who had carried the body that day said in a hushed whisper.

"It *is* a tomb," came the answer, the speaker glaring through goggles at the body-carrier.

They fell silent as the sandstorm raged over the remaining floorboards above them, some wincing at the sound of creaking wood and the showers of sand that rained down on them. Nervous glances were thrown at the body, but no one said anything about it. No one ever discussed the body.

When the storm had passed, hushed and nervous hours of falling masonry later, they looked to each other, their eyes finally congregating on the largest man, the one who had swapped out his gas mask for a pair of goggles. He was the unofficial leader of the group and was the only one who had survived being on the outside during the assault, and he was the only one who had come knocking on the government facility's door in the aftermath.

"We'll stay here tonight and sleep. O-five hundred tomorrow we're back on the road."

They all nodded. No one bothered to mention that most of the roads were gone, covered by sand or destroyed completely. Each man found a corner in which to set up a sleeping bag. Unconsciously each spot was as far from the body as safety would allow. Each man lay awake for hours, silent in the creaking hours of shadows. The only light came from the dying embers of the fire, the glow rendering the darkness much more horrifying than it already was. The groan of the building around them and the shrieking of the night wind were the only sounds besides the hissing patter of falling sand on cinderblocks.

"There's no rats," one of the congregation whispered fearfully and the others answered him with a stony silence.

The Leader, for that was what he had come to be known as since they had left the safety of the government facility, stared into the fire while the men slept. After walking for what felt like forever, they found what was left of a city, judging by the size of the foundation in which they set up camp. The rest of the building had either caved or was mostly blown away in the final war.

The fire snapped and crackled before him, but provided him no warmth. He searched through his breast pocket for the picture he kept next to his heart, and stared at it for a long time. He could no longer remember the name of the woman in the picture, and he was no longer sure he wanted to remember. To name her would acknowledge that she was gone, along with the rest of them. He allowed himself only to remember that he had loved her. As much as he had been able to love someone, anyway. He would never love another. There were no women left.

The fire sank lower into embers and he threw some of civilization's remnants onto the flames. A book that had been broken into kindling caught quickly, spreading flames to some dry-rotted children's toys, and in a few moments the fire was glowing strong.

"Where the hell did we go wrong?" he whispered hoarsely.

He tried to sigh, but only managed to suck dust deep into his lungs. With a choking cough he spat into the dirt, clearing sand from his throat and chest. The silence was broken only by the howl of the sandstorm raging around the building. Every night seemed to be marked by sandstorms, he thought. The world had gotten worse since he had left his fallout shelter in New Jersey and made the trek to Raven Rock. Cities that had been recognizable mere weeks before were covered in sand and torn up at the foundations. His initial optimism that they could save the world was as faded as the fallen bricks littering the basement floor.

He no longer expected answers. He stared at the sleeping men, their uniforms grayed and their medals tarnished. There were gaps where some of the medals had fallen off and been forgotten, and some of the stripes flapped their corners loosely in the dusty glow from the fire. He shifted his gaze to the rumpled shape on a stretcher they carried with them. The only one among them who had answers was under that dirt-encrusted canvas, he thought bitterly.

Sand ran through the cracks of the caved floor above them, piling onto the covered body as if to say time was running out. There was nothing left in the world but this group of men that he hated with all of his heart. He took out his gun and stared at the black metal of the barrel, feeling its weight like gravity in his hands. He held it out in front of him, aiming at each of his sleeping brothers of the apocalypse. It would be a mercy, he thought, doing them a favor even. They may even stay asleep after the first shot, sleep through the whole thing.

There was an ugly clattering sound when the muzzle bumped his teeth, and the taste was like coming home. He breathed in slowly, trying to stop his hand from shaking. With each breath he could taste fired shots and mayhem, oil and war.

Tears streaked muddy rivers down his cheeks when he thought of the ocean he had lived near, and how it had looked when he had before he had joined the mission. He had loved the ocean. What he had left behind was no longer the Atlantic Ocean. It had been quicksand with tides and the uncanny ability to kill anything that got too close to it. He wished he could see the ocean just once more the way it had been before all the bullshit went down.

He let his breath out slowly and caressed the trigger. The metal was cold, unyielding. There were so many things he could regret if he allowed himself to feel again. There were so many reasons to do this, and yet he had yet to fire that final shot.

"Fuckit," he whispered around the muzzle and closed his eyes in anticipation of the last thing he would hear.

One of the men stirred and he paused. Finally, he opened his eyes. He stared across the shelter to the body under the canvas shroud once more. Slowly, he lowered the gun back into his lap, watching the firelight flicker in the dull gunmetal.

He decided that he could think about eating his gun once the mission was complete. Afterall, he was the only one who really understood what the hell was going on in this newly made shit-hole of a world. He would lead them all from here to eternity if necessary. And when it was all over, he had to make sure that the body they were carrying stayed dead.

CHAPTER 7

When morning came many of the group were already awake, waiting to begin, to leave, to move on. To search for an end to the waking nightmare they moved through day by day. To continue the search for an elusive goal.

Beneath the caked and hollow lines of their hardened eyes they wore dark circles, the signs that they were haunted men. None of them dared mention that for months now there had been no sign of life-givers. No women. No children. No animals. Only hardened and haunted men on the move, all of them searching until they had forgotten what it was they were looking for.

The largest man, the leader, rose to his feet and the dirty-blonde bristles of his knife-chopped crewcut brushed the rotted boards of the ceiling above his head, sending down a fine powder of plaster and sand onto his shoulders in a man-made dandruff. His eyes were cold as he scanned the men around him, a faded blue, what the color of the Atlantic Ocean had once been before it had turned to quicksand. His thousand-yard stare looked through his company and silently they gathered up the body and moved on, leaving behind no trace of their having been there. Just in case there was still an enemy left alive.

They squinted against the glare as they resurfaced, each man training his stare ahead of him and never around him, afraid to look too closely at the toll of progress. Combat boots crunched over what was left of pavement, glass, and neighborhoods as they made their way out of the city's center, to the North and east, the body held stiffened and reeking on a stretcher between the two men whose duty it was to bear it that day.

The leader consulted a parched piece of paper, then looked to a broken map and compass. He scanned the horizon, the dirt on his weathered face cracking into a leathery frown. He could feel the expectant stares of his men, and he swallowed in preparation of the lie he would tell them. The same lie he told them every day.

"It's that way," he said, and pointed.

The compass said north no matter which way he turned it. It had been reading north for the past twenty miles, and had read north since they had started their journey. The men knew the lie and nodded their agreement. It was better than acknowledging what they all knew. The compass wasn't broken, the earth was.

Silently they trudged over the sands, the wind broken occasionally by a hacking cough and the wet smack of phlegm hitting the ground. The body smelled worse. Its scent carried on the wind, and the leader scanned the skies and ground for scavengers that would follow the scent of death, but there was nothing. His frown deepened to a scowl, every instinct telling him it wasn't right, that there were *always* scavengers to clean up the dead. Except there was nothing. Not another living thing. They had yet to even see a cockroach.

He glared over his shoulder at the body, loathing what it had contained before it had become their cross to bear. Suit, Highstrung, and Thinker had not told any of them *who* the body was, and gave strict orders not to find out, but he could guess. Only one person would have been so important.

Memories filtered through and his scowl deepened. Once he had lived by the ocean, in a small town that had been beaten to gray clapboards by sea air and winter storms. It had been a peaceful and lonely existence, and he had enjoyed it. Somehow he had known it would never last. The man the body had once contained was responsible for the demise of any semblance of normal life. Any *chance* at normal life. The actions taken had been carried away by obsession and power, and the earth had paid the price for human frailty.

He pulled back from his musings and glanced around at his men, loathing them for their dependence on his decisions, but it had been *their* idea to carry the body. He had agreed, turning them toward the ocean, to where the ocean *should* have been. When they had reached the coast there was nothing but heaving sand washing onto a glass shore.

They had lost one of their number that day, a man by the name of Smith who had refused to listen to the leader's words of caution and wandered too close to that churning mass of so much dirt. His combat boots had crunched through the layer of beach glass as he walked toward what had been the Atlantic Ocean, his eyes wide and staring with shock. Smith's screams had been mercifully short-lived when the ocean had pulled him under.

"Sir?"

The cold eyes of the leader settled onto the man who had interrupted the memory. He shook off the shiver of revulsion and fear, setting his jaw to that of the trained killer he had once been.

The man fell in step with him, his voice low as he cast a furtive glance back at the rest of the company. The leader looked to the name stenciled on the man's jacket pocket: Jenkins.

"Sir," Jenkins began again, "Where are we going? What exactly is it that we're looking for?"

The leader glared at Jenkins. "That is on a need to know basis, soldier, and classified information."

Jenkins glared at him. "With all due respect, *sir*, just where the fuck do you think you are??" He motioned to everything around them. "It's *over*. There's no more secrets to protect. We won, for what *that's* worth."

The leader regarded him for a moment. He almost smiled, remembering a time not long ago when he himself had said almost the same words to an uptight asshole in a suit.

"You know the name of what we're looking for, and you know why we're looking for it. That's all I know, too."

Jenkins let out a snort of exasperation and threw an angry glance back to the body.

"I say we bury him wherever. He's dead, he won't mind, and we can move a hell of a lot faster to find whatever it is we're looking for without the deadweight."

With a motion smooth and almost unconscious, the gun was pulled and fired into Jenkins' head. The leader watched as the look of shock melted to blood and gore during Jenkins' descent to the ground. He turned to look at the rest of the men, his expression hard and unreadable as his eyes stared through each of them.

"Any other questions?" he asked quietly.

The others shook their heads.

"Good. Bury Jenkins and let's go."

Two of the company broke off and with shovels cracked through the dry earth until a hole roughly the size of their fallen comrade was ready. With an air of solemnity they pushed the fresh body into the hole and covered it with dead earth, then resumed their posts carrying the long-dead body on its stretcher.

Looks were thrown between some of the men, but no one would say anything more about their mission or the insanity of it. Not out loud. Not when they were so unsure of the reaction it would win them. They stared at the broad shoulders of their leader, his faded fatigues, and his cracked combat boots. Before they had ever met him he had removed the stencil of his name from his clothing with bleach and sandpaper. No one could remember how he had become the commander of the group, but there he was, leading them on a mission on which he hadn't even really wanted to join them.

Over the course of a week a few more of their number were buried after the Jenkins incident. Some took their own lives, and some had theirs taken.

CHAPTER 8

On what would have been a Sunday, they came to a clearing in the sandy wasteland. He stared in disbelief, thinking it a mirage.

He heard the awe in his voice as he whispered, "It *does* exist."

The men rushed forward, almost ecstatic to see green that wasn't the color of sandblasted fatigues or faded camouflage. They knelt to touch the grass that sprang forth from rich soil, marveling at the delineation where sand became earth. They plunged their hands into clear streams of water and drank, happy to taste only water and not the metallic inside of a canteen.

He approached them, fighting his own excitement, and told them, "We still have a mission to accomplish, men. Let's get it done."

He motioned to those who still carried the body to join them, then motioned for everyone to gather around him.

"OK. We accomplished the first half of the directive, which was to find the Lazarus Stone, and judging from our surroundings, I would say we're damn close. Once we find it and get it into the ocean, this thing should do whatever it is that it does…."

They all looked around them, concern suddenly written across each man's face, each one of them very much aware of exactly what the stone did, and what they intended to use it for. They had spent what felt like years searching for it under the belief that they would never find it, but it gave their lives purpose to continue a futile search in a dead world. Now that they had found it, they began to doubt their resolve to actually use it. Some things were better off dead.

"What does it look like, sir? Where should we start to look?" one of the men asked.

He scanned their surroundings and contemplated the question. His eyes squinted to cold slits and then he raised an accusing finger towards the middle of the undergrowth.

"The growth pattern is circular, so let's start at the center."

With a collective shiver in the heat of the day they followed the leader toward the heart of the growth, the greenery becoming more lush and abundant as they moved inward. As they came closer to the center they could just make out a dull glow beneath the earth, illuminating the overgrown grass and weeds from below like a B-Movie science experiment.

"There it is!" one of the men shouted, removing his sand-blasted goggles and letting out a hoarse laugh that was near to hysteria.

"Right," the leader said quietly.

He turned to face the men, scanning them for a general idea of the collective mood. They were afraid. Each man stood uneasily, faded fatigues hanging loosely on near-skeletal frames, their hollow eyes both hopeful and wild with their terror at the unknown. He motioned to one of the men holding the stretcher to join him. He scanned the nametag on the man's fatigues before addressing him.

"What do you think, Harris?"

Harris pulled his eyes away from the subterranean glow and glanced over his shoulder at the others, then back to the leader. He tried to smile, only exposing the remains of broken, rotted teeth and the gaps that had been left behind by prior broken rotted teeth.

"What do I think about what, sir?" he asked, keeping his voice neutral and his eyes fixed on the horizon.

His voice cracked on the last word as the leader turned to face him. For the first time since he had joined them the leader smiled. It was a horrible sight.

"We need to test it. Don't you think? Make sure it does what it's supposed to do."

The soldier nodded slowly, searching for the meaning behind the leader's words. Looking for the catch that would end his hellish existence. At least it would be quick, he thought with relief.

"Thank you for volunteering."

Harris didn't have time to protest his own death when the leader shot him. The others flinched angrily, but fear kept their outrage silent. Instead they watched the body fall, watched the leader dig a shallow grave over the glow, watched him kick their fallen comrade into the hole then cover him.

Minutes passed in silence after the last handful of dirt had been thrown on top of Harris. The men stood around the mound, unsure of what exactly they waited for, but waiting nonetheless. Finally their hated leader broke the silence, a manic grin spread over his face as he pointed to the hole.

"There! Look!"

The dirt began to move, slowly at first, and then frantically as Harris sucked dirt into his lungs and struggled to free himself from the earth. He sat up with a hollow groan and coughed mud onto the ground around him, then looked at the leader. Hate filled his gaze and he struggled to his feet, stumbling toward the man that had killed and resurrected him back into perdition.

"Damn you!" he cried hoarsely, fingers reaching forward, clawing the air before him.

"I already am," the leader's smile broadened, "We all are."

Harris was still too slow on his feet to avoid being clothes-lined. With a smooth and practiced motion the leader dropped to his knee beside the fallen man and snapped his neck. The others stared in horror, but no one said anything as their leader got to his feet and motioned to the body.

"Alright, men, let's bury him."

"With all due respect, sir, wouldn't burying Harris only bring him back again?"

Atlantic blue eyes glared through the speaker for a moment and then the leader let out a hearty laugh. He pointed to the soldier and nodded.

"You know, I hadn't thought of that!"

His mirth was short-lived, however. The gravity of the situation and the mission settled over him and the frown quickly chased the smile. He gazed at the men, his face once more unreadable. The diminished troop watched him warily, a select few moved their hands almost imperceptibly to their guns.

The leader took a deep breath and let it out slowly, eyes closed and body open to his surroundings. With set jaw he began to shoot the remainder of the men. None of them fired a single shot, even the ones who had had the foresight to reach for their guns. On a basic level, they all knew he would do this to them, and some even went so far as to welcome death when it came for them.

When it was over, and the last man had fallen, he opened his eyes to assess the amount of carnage he had caused. He was glad to see that none of the men looked surprised. They probably suspected his plan all along, and knew that they would be obligated to stop him had they been alive when the time came to carry it out. Or maybe they would have planned to do the same thing if they had been in his place.

As he stood among his fallen former comrades he reached a shaking hand into his breast pocket and took out a crumpled, weather-beaten piece of paper. The ink was faded, but most of the handwriting was still visible across the photograph. He scanned it briefly, his jaw clenched and throat working against the cry of anguish that tried to escape him. Despite his training, years of combat, and countless medals of honor, nothing could have prepared any man for what had happened to the world. He kissed the paper, holding it to his lips as tears tracked their way through the dust on his cheeks.

"You were right…. But I never thought I would see the day…," he whispered, smiling through his tears as he put the paper back into his pocket.

He dug a new grave, this one slightly deeper than the one he had dug for Harris. When it was deep enough he moved to the stretcher and pushed the canvas-wrapped body into the hole. His eyes were feverish as he filled in the grave, and his breathing was jagged with excitement as he waited, kneeling before the mound of earth.

When the dirt began to shift he willed himself to remain calm. There came a hollow, dirt-filled moan as the man sat up, and loose soil spilled across the canvas shroud as it unwrapped and peeled away from the lapels of the man's crumpled suit. He wiped at his eyes and then looked around him. The signs of decay were already retreating from his face until it seemed as if he had never been dead. He climbed from his shallow grave unsteadily, trying to both regain his balance and dust himself off. He started in surprise when his eyes met the cold gaze of the leader.

"Hello, son," the man said with a smile as white and complete as it had been the day he died. "I assume I have you to thank for this."

The leader gave a nod and got to his feet. He stood at attention and waited for the man to finish getting himself together. The man brushed dirt from his suit, pulling his pants up a little higher over his beer belly.

"Well, you have my undying gratitude, ...?" The man faltered, his hand outstretched and ready for the handshake as his eyes searched the uniform for any indication of name or military rank and branch.

The leader gave a tight-lipped smile. "I don't have a name anymore, sir. I haven't had one for some time."

"Ahh.... I can respect that," the man said with a hint of well-hidden unease beneath a southern good ole boy drawl. He looked around them and turned back to the leader. "Refresh my memory... what happened?" the man asked. He had not yet noticed the group of bodies surrounding him.

The smile flitted away from the leader's mouth. "How do you mean, sir?"

The man motioned to their surroundings and to the desert beyond the oasis. "Why are we in the desert?"

"It's all that's left, sir."

The man contemplated the statement until slow realization dawned in his faded hazel eyes. His face paled and he put his hand to his forehead as he fumbled to a sitting position on the ground.

"My God…. Oh, my God. What have I done?"

The man looked up at the leader, tears streaming down his face. "Where is everyone else? Were there any survivors?"

"There were some survivors. We carried you to the Lazarus Stone."

"Where are these brave men and women now?" the man asked.

The leader shook his head. "No women, sir. Only men. We haven't seen a woman in quite some time."

"No women…? But my wife, my mother….daughters and granddaughters….?"

"Gone, sir."

The man climbed to his feet. His face was ashen as he scrutinized the leader's expressionless face. "Did you lose anyone, son?"

"Yes, sir," the leader said and his voice cracked with the agony of holding back a flood of emotion as he touched his breast pocket where the crumbled photograph hid.

"Wife?"

The leader shook his head. "She was someone I loved too much to ever admit it. Even to her."

The man nodded his gray head and straightened his suit as he straightened his back, looking around him. Finally his eyes fell on the bodies.

"What the hell happened here?" he asked incredulously.

The leader glanced to the men he had murdered and sighed. "I gave them their honorable discharge, sir."

The man spun angrily back to the leader, eyes furious and fearful. "Why in God's name would you do something like that?"

"Because, sir, this has been hell. I hope where they are now they might have found something closer to heaven, or at least peace."

The man took a deep breath and adjusted his suit again in pure politician style. Almost unconsciously he began to nod.

"We can do this, you and me. We can get the world back in order, start over. Right, soldier?"

The leader looked at the man in disbelief, shorter and slighter of frame than he was, looking at him hopefully with shifty eyes. The man had no idea the sacrifices that had been made, the lives lost. Death had helped him forget the hard lessons that they had all learned.

"I can't let you do that, sir," he said sadly.

The man glared at him, a child preparing to throw a tantrum. "What do you mean you can't *let* me? Are you not a soldier? Did you not take an oath to protect this nation?"

"I was a soldier, and was forced to become a soldier again after I had long laid down my rifle. I never wanted to see what

I've seen, and I never wanted to have to bury my entire family due to someone getting their panties in a bunch because they didn't have enough power," the leader removed his gun from its holster and pointed it at the man before him, "I *am* protecting this nation, sir. I just wanted you to know that I completed the mission you gave us."

The gunshot rang through the silence, the bullet tearing through scalp and bone. The leader watched the body fall to the ground with a sense of sadness. So many lives had been wasted.

Numbness settled over him as he dragged the bodies away from the circle of growth and buried them in the cracked sand of the desert. Absently he kicked sand over the blood trails of his men as he returned to the oasis, to the center. He stared down at the dull glow beneath the earth for a moment, then dropped to his knees and began to dig.

The glow brightened as he released the stone from the earth, the smooth polished surface cool in his fingers as he held it. It filled most of his grasping hands, surprisingly heavy, perfectly oblong, the glow swirling a pale unnatural pastel green inside the stone. The light reflected in his staring eyes, illuminating the morbid fascination that hid in their depths.

He placed the stone in his pack and began to walk back across the sand, toward where he remembered the ocean to be. He vaguely wondered if it would still be there, or if it had dried up since he had last seen it.

Days passed, possibly weeks, and still he walked. He had finished what was left of his rations, and was down to the last drops of water when he recognized the sound of the ocean just over a set of dunes.

The leader began to run, a hoarse laugh ripping from his parched lips as he saw the waves of sand. His face cracked into a smile as he reached into his pack to retrieve the Lazarus Stone, clutching it in hands that were numb with anticipation and fatigue. He fumbled in his pocket and removed the faded photograph, holding it against his heart as he ran. His combat boots cracked through the hardened beach as he approached the waves, stripping off his pack, his jacket, and his shirt until he stood half naked. When he came closer, he sat down to remove his combat boots and fatigues, leaving a trail of clothing that had once had his name stenciled across the pockets and now contained a faded bleach stain where his name had been.

Clutching the stone in his hands, he approached the crashing waves, then threw with all of his remaining strength. He watched the stone as it sailed through the air, end over end, until it was swallowed by the waves.

Within minutes water was crashing back onto the shore, and he fell to the cracked beach with a sigh of relief. He began to dig, punching through the hardened sand until his knuckles and wrists bled, until he had a hole that was roughly his size and shape. The effort took much of his strength, and he rested in the hole, propped up by the mound of sand he had removed from the beach.

The ocean was turning the color of clean water, the beach glass cracking beneath the churning surf. The leader was sure that within days the growth would begin, and the earth would heal itself.

He held the photograph up to the fading embers of sunset, the woman in the picture gone now. Her dark hair obscured parts of her face, but her eyes were visible, looking out of the photo, looking at him. Smiling. She had tried to help him long ago, had even tried to love him, and he had pushed her away. The photo had arrived at his address the day before the end of the world, with the simple words written across the bottom: "You will save the world."

He rested his head against the pile of sand and watched the ocean heal itself. She had been right.

He released his last breath as night fell. When morning came the ocean was once more the same color as his open eyes.

EPILOGUE: THE END OF THE BEGINNING

*Excerpt from journal retrieved from apartment on 3rd and South Streets,
Philadelphia, PA:*

Strange day…. My cat has been acting weirder than usual and
won't let me out of his sight. It's like he's waiting for something. The
even weirder part is that I feel kind of the same way, as if something
BIG was about to happen. As if to confirm this feeling, my phone's
touch screen has stopped working when I touch it. It's not just me,
either. I stopped in at the bar downstairs on my way out to take a
walk and had my friend try it out. It worked fine for him, but not for
me. It's like I wasn't touching it at all.

At about noon a call came in with an unknown number.
When I picked up the phone it answered itself and went straight to
speaker. The words were not in English or any language I had ever
heard, but somehow I understood. I was going to be late if I didn't
hurry.

I came back home after that and my cat was practically
frantic. I finally had to put him in his carrier so he'd calm down a

little. I have him next to me as I write this, which seems to help. I feel strange, though, as if my body were breaking down on a molecular level. I feel like I could fly apart at any minute…. Whatever it is my feline friend and I have been waiting for, it's here. At last something is

THE WORLD IS WAITING FOR THE SUNRISE

By XIRCON

It's been days since we saw a bed and a hot meal. We've trekked across the United States, back to the east coast. To home. None of us was sure what we would find once we got to the West Coast, but it wasn't much. Life was subjective there to begin with, and after the end it only got worse. I had hoped to find friends there, but found only heartache and ruin.

Joe lights up a cigarette, pulling me out of my mental wanderings, and Jenna coughs with purpose. Joe ignores her and inhales deeply. Jenna grabs the cigarette from his fingers on the exhale and places it between her own lips.

"That was my last one," Joe sulks.

Jenna lets out a little smoke-filled sigh then shoves the cigarette back into Joe's pouting lips.

"Quit yer bitchin.' I just wanted a drag."

She turns back to the road and pulls her mittens back on, then adjusts her scarf and coat. Others join us along the way, and we walk on in companionable silence.

"What do you think it'll be like when we get there?" one kid asks.

I glance over at him. He can't be more than sixteen, but he's got that look of hope and immortality that all kids his age have. I give a shrug, but before I can answer Joe starts in on his story.

"Gonna be amazing," he says, "Got a cigarette? I'll tell you what it's like."

The kid fishes through his jacket pockets and finally frees a crumpled pack of cigarettes. He hands one to Joe. Joe lights it up and inhales like he's sucking down friggin' manna from heaven.

He exhales and the smoke curls around us in the darkness like a specter of a time long past. Joe reverently waits for it to dissipate before speaking.

"First, it's like everywhere else, you know? Dark. But then there's this spark just over the trees and in a few minutes you don't even need a flashlight no more."

The kid stares at Joe, his face lit with rapt attention and reflected flashlight illumination. He pulls out a cigarette for himself and Joe holds out his lighter for the kid. Jenna lets out a cough and Joe hands her the cigarette from his own lips before she has a chance to take a forcible drag.

"Where you from originally?" Joe asks the kid.

"Montana," the kid says shyly and drops his gaze to the ground as he pulls another inhale.

"No shame in that," Joe says and Jenna's snort of derision cancels out his goodwill.

The kid coughs and shifts uneasily under Jenna's glare. She really is the headkill of the trip, I muse.

"I'm from New York," I tell anyone who cares to listen.

My words silence the group and they stare at me for what I am: a dying species. A myth and a thing of legend.

"Is it true you could dance in a church?" one kid asks.

I nod.

"And you could smoke in the clubs and restaurants?"

Again, I nod.

The group stares in amazement. "And transfats?"

"All over the place," I say with a nostalgic sigh, "before they started to poison us, that is."

"What about the water?"

"Un-medicated, except for fluoride and chlorine in the city."

A collective gasp goes up and I feel old suddenly. These kids have no idea what it was like to drink fresh city water without a prescription in it or watch a television that had no subliminal messaging system already built into it.

By the time we reach the east coast there are over 1,000 of us. We line up along the edge of the piers and waterfronts at Exchange Place in Jersey City and wait, staring in rapt silence at the New York skyline towering over the Hudson River.

"Now what?" Jenna whispers.

"We wait," Joe tells her.

A cop wanders by and considers the crowd of us lining the waterfront. He clears his throat and glares at Joe's cigarette.

"Any reason you're all out here in the freezing cold and smoking?"

The group looks to me for an explanation and I find myself at a loss for words in the face of authority. I shrug and pull a black clove cigarette from my coat pocket. The taste of the filter is nothing short of honey-dipped heaven, the heady stale aroma already permeating the air around me.

"You can't smoke that," the cop tells me, pointing to the clove cigarette like it's a grenade and I smile tight-lipped around the smoking black cylinder.

"We're waiting for the sunrise, officer," I tell him.

His eyes widen in something akin to fear. "No one waits for the sunrise, kids," he warns, "Everyone knows it's dangerous."

I shrug and pull another drag. "We're not here to hurt anyone, sir. We're just here to watch the first light."

The cop snorts and walks away shaking his head. We can hear him mutter, "Your funeral."

Joe pulls at my sleeve. "What's he mean by that?"

I stare at the skyline. "He means not everyone makes it."

Jenna's anxious face joins Joe's. "WE are gonna make it, right?"

"You have to want to make it. There can't be an ounce of doubt," I tell them.

We wait the rest of the time in silence. Some of the kids get spooked last minute and run for cover. I stand my ground, and I'm happy to see Joe and Jenna standing next to me. We grasp hands and wait, seeing the first hint of the sun between the buildings that loom over the frozen Hudson River.

"I'm scared," Jenna says suddenly breaking the silence.

"Shhh," I tell her, "You're going to love it on the other side."

As the sun hits us full on I can hear the gasps and cries from the group, the shouts of joy and wonder. I open my eyes, not realizing I had closed them at some point, and stare onto the restored skyline. The Twin Towers gleam in the sunrise, reflecting into an unfrozen river. The city is waking up, and the scent of fried foods and carnival festivity gathers on the breeze and reaches us.

"Where are we?" Joe asks.

"Home," I say to him and to those that have made it past the fear and doubt and followed me blindly to a better time and place.

THE MONSTER UNDER THE BED

By James Glass

Some have called me a savior and others a demon. Regardless of names, I have a function, and I love my job. For those who hate the ones I torment, I am a nothing less than a lesser deity, karma in action. For those I visit - shall we call them victims? - I am nothing less than hell and nothing more than magnified guilt.

For your consideration, this sleeping beauty stretched out before me. Women are easy targets, statistics and studies don't have to tell you that. Plant a few seeds throughout the formative years: a noise in the closet, a scratching in the walls, and before long your cheeky little girl will blossom into a lovely, terrified woman.

In fact, it's even better if she's pretty. There will be so much more for her to fear. Aging, rape, abusive lovers and husbands, the nagging sense that no one will ever take her seriously... and then I saunter in, give them a kiss, and terrorize the holy hell out of them.

It can be as subtle as a wink through their own reflection in the mirror or as prolonged and complicated as our sleeping princess. To the casual observer she is merely having a bad dream. I know better because I know my work. She has been a project of mine since long before her first illicit affair. Look beneath the moans and eyelids to the dream. It's my personal favorite. She's had it for so long that she's growing to like it, and that terrifies her more than her fear of me.

There is a level of control in dreams by the dreamer, but look at all these chains and straps she's created to bind herself. Escape is not an option and she knows it. Despite that knowledge, she struggles fantastically. Observe how her body pulls against its bonds, a naked art in motion. Makes me want to skip the foreplay sometimes, but what kind of monster would I be if I did that?

Watch how she tenses when I slide my fingers across her naked flesh. When her eyes open wide, awake and staring up at me I tell her the same thing I tell her every night before I make her scream....

"It's just me...."

THE PREACHINGS OF MR. MINISTRY

By Mr. Ministry

PSALM I

Something… thinking something not right… got the beat and I'm dancing to it, across the cross-fade bass-boosting my soul to humility.

Watched too much TV

The radon filled the screams, saw the aliens running in the burning streets burning books for fun and profit

Control the liquid assets

Kill the cause of will

Firing at freedom

Perform perform perform! Screamed the Tick Tock Jock Men marching through time and

Control! Controlling liquid gardens

Killing Kill Kill KILL your televisions

Mindless sheep weep as they're herded to Slaughterhouse 5

Laughter following on the oil-sludged heels of the damned

Control the killing cause freedom of will speech babble offending
prerogative

Machine-gunning poets and artists and word-writers,

controlling the media

unleashing the paparazzi onto innocent trespassers

Despise your fellow man, trip to the MOON, you assholes

smoking cancer Styx burning lives to ashes to ashes and dust to dust,
but we love you so we get rid of you—get away RUN! It's the only
way. Heed the words and get out!

GET OUT!

It's the only way. Leave this hellhole while you still can

Burn the bitches! Tie them all to Vegan steaks and BURN!

Burn your bridges before you cross them, set the ones you love on
fire and light up the sky

GET OUT!

And take them all with you....

PSALM II

Waste the youth

Kill the elders too

Shifting in their sunken-grave taped-up eyes,

you're crazy and I'm committing crazy things

Sticking pins and needles into open eyes that have seen the light

Running razors over wrists

Draining life over the razorwires, over chainlinks

Life is only strong as a weakened chainlink fence topped in barbed
wire

Tearing eyes out to get to the soul

Opening the windows and swallowing hole

Spring cleaning the mind by pumping the veins with poison,
bleaching the blemishes and scars away

Staring up at the sky, mouth agape and wonder why....

PSALM III

Listen to the rivers running red to the fix

Getting fixed with mantras of "Just one" No one will ever know…
one little bleeding heart dying in the snow.

Kill those bastitches

breaking skulls with weighted aluminum litanies of rage

and off to Napalm Sunday Elysian Fields

Remember the bad old days they just got worse

War and death and love of fear, the backyard Barbie-Q and a cold can of beer scorching the throat, burning the eyes

Melting a face and slashing the cries—die

Sailing down the red rivers into icy eyes staring up and open on bathroom tiles

Crashing red Deadhead

Bloodlines making up a suicide sketch of murder portrait photography artist studio.

PSALM IV

Darkest hours filled

With quiet dawn tick-tocking

Clocks of time staring in veins

Pulsing blue serge minds exploding

With new thoughts to suppress listen to the liars

Lying in weight for the truth

A list controls my life

With subsistence not inexistence

Oh yeah, PC to PVC

Vinyl screaming for the Vinyl Mistress

Oh yeah

Oh yeah

Drowning in the Life

Oh yeah, stab at Life with needle-veins and fuck the sky

We're going to the MOON

Surging forward pulling back always backward

Look at the blind future world with out ends world within dyes

Spirit holes

Bleeding faith onto cold concrete-hard fact

Twist in oil and gold and rust

Polish the chrome with blood and tears

Songs of rust and chrome to dust

Ashes on ashes churning to burning the trust

Shooting nostalgia with stingers and blame

Staring lifeless sunken-grave eyes

Staring into the dream

PSALM V

Scratch at your faces

Tearing out that one good eye blind

Taped eyes staring out at the cold cruel world

Dear God what have you become

Don't ask questions that answer crucifixion

Nail bombed hands and wrists and ankles bleeding hearts for humanity

Resent those that have covered you in stitches

Bingeing alcoholics rotting in bars with cells for filthy bathrooms

Racing roaches in business suits

It's too early to be too late

Bodies floating to the surface of society bloated and gasping with undeath

Sucking the life from love

Blaspheming with their glances, empty sockets staring where eyes should have been

Empty souls gaping like open graves yawning black and six feet deep

Pushing in and burning the bitches

Mass grave mentality with mob morality nailing values in one Christ at a time

Over 100 billion served! Stay out of the sun look longer live younger

Vampires with notched-up wrists

The road to Hell's been paved with good inventions

Pushers paved the asphalt to Heaven and millions have scorched their feet to firewalk it

Who said the best things in life are free?

Pay it with blood.

Your credit's always good here.

OTHER WORKS BY THE AUTHOR

THE IMMORTAL WAR SERIES
NEMESIS (Book 1)

LAMIA (Book 2)

THE TOWER (Book 3)

SECOND-HAND SARAH

THE MURDERED METATRON (release date: July 2013)

CONVERSATIONS WITH A DEMON (release date: Fall 2013)

Writing as XIRCON:

IN THE HANGING CAGES

ADDITIONAL SHORT STORIES AND NOVELLAS CAN BE FOUND AT THE AUTHOR'S AMAZON PAGE:
http://www.amazon.com/Suzi-M/e/B003TTLGP2/ref=ntt_athr_dp_pel_pop_1

Works of XIRCON can be found on Amazon at:
http://www.amazon.com/Xircon-Z/e/B005N099QS/ref=sr_ntt_srch_lnk_1?qid=1371586243&sr=1-1

45472053R00099

Made in the USA
Middletown, DE
05 July 2017